DISCARD

My Brothers' Keeper

My Brothers' Keeper

A Civil War Story

By

Nancy Johnson

DOWN EAST BOOKS
Camden / Maine

Text copyright © 1997 by Nancy W. Johnson
Jacket illustration © 1997 by Jim Sollers
ISBN 0-89272-414-5 (hardcover)
ISBN 0-89272-433-1 (softcover)

Printed and bound at Thomson-Shore, Inc.

2   4   6   8   9   7   5   3   1

Down East Books
P.O. Box 679, Camden, Maine 04843
Book Orders: 1-800-766-1670

Library of Congress Cataloging-in-Publication Data

Johnson, Nancy, 1933-
        My brothers' keeper : a Civil War story / by Nancy Johnson.
            p.   cm.
        Summary: As a young orphaned drummer boy in the Civil War, Josh
    Parish joins the 20th Maine in time to be caught up in the battle for Little
    Round Top.
        ISBN 0-89272-414-5 (hardcover)
        ISBN 0-89272-433-1 (softcover)
        1. United States—History—Civil War, 1861–1865—Juvenile fiction.
    2. Gettysburg (Pa.), Battle of, 1863—Juvenile fiction. [1. United States—
    History—Civil War, 1861–1865—Fiction. 2. Gettysburg (Pa.), Battle of,
    1863—Fiction.] I. Title.
    PZ7.J63417My   1997
    [Fic]—dc21
                                                                    97-27186
                                                                         CIP
                                                                          AC

For my husband

Contents

AUTHOR'S NOTE

MY mother first read my great, great uncles' letters to me when I was ten. She kept them in a black tin box decorated with gold scrolls and flowers and hearts. The letter paper was tissue thin, yellowed, and worn where it had been folded and refolded.

Mother told me the story of these two Rochester, New York, brothers, who went to war in 1861. They wrote letters home to their family telling about the everyday things that happened to them in the Union Army. She had a picture of one brother, a handsome young man with dark hair and light eyes. I was heartbroken when I learned he had been killed, still a teenager, in an ambush in Virginia.

I read and reread the letters my distant uncles had written, and I imagined them, as they described themselves, strolling the streets of Harper's Ferry "with a loaf of bread under each arm, and each eating a pancake." One uncle wrote that he had passed through the back streets of Alexandria, where he "saw a building three stories high built of brick with the sign Price Birch & Co. Dealer in Slaves." It was something different from anything he had seen before, he said.

I think I knew then that someday I would write about these brothers. With my husband's help, I have researched the life and times of the Union soldiers in the Civil War. This book, *My Brothers' Keeper: A Civil War Story,* is part fact, part fiction, and part the story of my great, great uncles. I hope my young readers will realize that all of us have a story somewhere in our lives, a story that just needs telling.

—Nancy Johnson

FOREWORD

In 1860, Abraham Lincoln ran for president. He denounced the practice of slavery as evil and vowed that the United States would not be divided. When Lincoln was elected in November, the country knew there would be war.

Demanding the right to own slaves, South Carolina seceded from the Union in December 1860. Ten more states joined South Carolina to form the Confederate States of America.

On April 12, 1861, Confederate soldiers fired on United States Army troops at Fort Sumter on the South Carolina coast, and the American Civil War began.

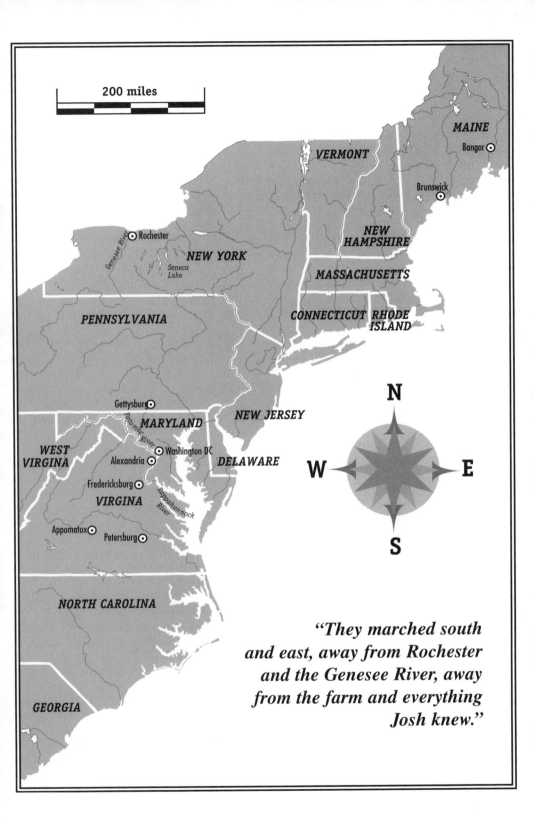

"They marched south and east, away from Rochester and the Genesee River, away from the farm and everything Josh knew."

✯✯ *One* ✯✯

THE FARM

JOSH shivered and moved closer to his sister, Mattie. Behind him, Aunt Carrie sniffed as she squeezed his shoulder. Please don't do that, he cried silently. When you do that, more tears come out.

He looked sideways through a blur of tears at his brother, Jere, who stood tall and straight on the other side of Mattie. Why can't I be like that? He's not crying like a baby, Josh thought. He looked across the grave. The Man was staring at him with unseeing eyes.

The preacher's voice droned on and on, like flies down by the pond in summer. Raising his eyes, Josh watched a flock of Canada geese pierce the blue March sky and disappear over the bare treetops, flying north towards Lake Ontario. He shivered again. It would be several weeks still before the air warmed, bringing the vibrant green of spring to the trees and fields of western New York state.

His eyes were drawn back to the grave, dug with great difficulty in the still-frozen ground. With a steady *thump, thump,* men from the neighboring farms shoveled clods of cold earth onto his mother's casket. Don't watch, Josh begged, but he could not pull his eyes away.

When the men had finished, women laid branches of dried wildflowers on the mound of earth that swelled gently over the casket. The preacher led them in singing "Abide With Me," his robust voice drowning out the others, lingering over a long "Aaah-men." Then everyone shuffled awkwardly down the hill toward the farmhouse, which stood a little ways away.

"Poor younguns. They'll miss their mother."

"Do you suppose *he* will stay?"

"Well he has to, doesn't he?"

A bony woman in a shiny black bonnet spoke to Josh. "You need to look out for your sister now," she instructed him. Josh nodded.

1

"She should go and live with your aunt in Rochester. This is no place for an eleven-year-old girl, out here alone with that man and you two boys." Josh nodded again.

Stamping their feet, slapping their arms to warm themselves, the neighbors clustered on the porch that ran along the front side of the square, log farmhouse. They crowded inside the room, filling it, drawing the children in with them. The Man, who was the children's stepfather, hurried to the stone fireplace. He stirred up the dying fire, and soon the room grew bright and warmer.

Near the iron stove, a polished, oak table bulged with platters of ham and wild turkey, and crockery bowls filled with potatoes, hard-cooked eggs, spiced apples, and pickled beets. There were loaves of freshly baked bread and a plate of molasses cookies. On the stove, soup that smelled like herbs from the forest bubbled against the sides of a heavy kettle. Everyone who had come to the funeral had brought food. Now they ate and gossiped and consoled the family. Later, there would be plenty of food left over to last the family for a week or more.

"Come get some of this good ham," Aunt Carrie fussed, squeezing Josh's shoulder again.

Pulling away, Josh answered, "I'm not hungry." Then, remembering his manners, he added, "Thank you."

"You have to eat, boy," his uncle said, putting a friendly arm around Josh's shoulders.

It's better than being squeezed, Josh thought. "In a little while, sir. I'll eat in a little while," he answered.

"Good lad." His uncle smiled

Aunt Carrie caught Josh in her plump arms, squeezing him tightly. "You children can come and stay with us in Rochester," she whispered in his ear. A cozy feeling spread over Josh like the smell of his aunt's violet cologne. What a relief! Tears filled his eyes again, burning them, spilling down his cheeks. He hunched his shoulders and tried to slip away.

His uncle's friendly hand patted his shoulder as he said, "Put your shoulders back, Joshua. You have to act like a man. Look over there at Jere. See how tall he's standing. Try to be like Jere."

Josh stood as straight as he could and answered, "Yes, sir." Inside, he thought, I want to be like that only I just can't stop crying. I know I should be a man like Jere. I want to be, but how do I do it?

His uncle asked him, "How old are you now, Joshua?"

2

"I'm twelve, sir."

"You're not big like your brother, are you? He looks almost grown. What is he now, fifteen?"

"Fourteen, sir. He'll be fifteen next month."

Aunt Carrie interrupted them. "Do you think your stepfather will let you come to Rochester?"

Josh's shoulders sagged. He couldn't help it. The Man would never let them go. He needed them to work on the farm. "He won't let us go, not Jere and me, anyway. He might let you take Mattie," he explained to his aunt.

Aunt Carrie beamed. "We could take her back with us when we go tomorrow. That would be best for her, Joshua. You're very grown up to see that."

I don't see it, he protested, but silently. He knew Mattie *should* go; it was the right thing for her. Just before she died, his mother had said, "You must always search your heart for what is right for you to do, Joshua, and what is right for Mattie, too. She is too young to be left alone."

"I will," he promised, trying to comfort her.

"And your brother. You must try to keep him . . . to help him . . . He's so . . . so . . ."

"I know," Josh told her gently.

He had felt so helpless as his mother's life slipped away. All he could do was keep her clean and turn her in bed so she didn't get bedsores like old Mr. Hobbs, who lived on the next farm north. Josh read to his mother from the Bible as she had read to him when he was little. It eased the pain for both of them.

Mattie had tried to help, brushing her mother's hair into a dark fan across the pillow, holding a cup steady so she could take small sips of broth. As they cared for her, a bond grew between Josh and Mattie.

That will be spoiled if she goes to Rochester, Josh thought miserably. Oh, why do you think of yourself all the time? You know it's best for her to go. You promised Mother.

"You should take her," he gulped to Aunt Carrie, turning quickly away in case tears came again.

He noticed that a neighbor went to stand next to The Man by the fire, but The Man turned abruptly and left the house.

He did not have many friends among the other farmers. He had appeared one day six years ago, shortly after the children's father had been killed on a trip out West. Widow Parish had hired The Man to help out, and after a while he married her and took over the farm.

He was not deliberately cruel to the children; he just didn't like them very much. At first they were too small to be much help, getting in his way when he worked. He would hit at them to drive them away. Later, when he wanted Josh and Jere to help him stack hay in the barn or shuck corn to fill the corncrib, they did not want to come near him, so he hit at them to make them come.

He drank whiskey from a jug that he hid in the barn. Their mother had not liked it when he drank. His language became rough and he cuffed the boys or pinched Mattie for acting "silly." When Mama protested, he would sulk, going off to sleep in the barn and glowering at all of them the next day.

Soon the neighbors began to leave in little groups. They had to be home before dark to do chores. Murmuring words of sympathy to the children, they promised to come again. The Man had not returned.

When only Aunt Carrie and Uncle remained, Jere and Uncle went out to the barn to take care of the animals. Mattie took her mother's shawl from the spindle-backed rocker and sat near the fire with Aunt Carrie. Josh sat on his bed across the room, watching them.

"We should get some of these things packed away," Aunt Carrie said, opening the cedar chest that stood by the fireplace. She reached for the shawl to put it in, but Mattie drew back, wrapping the shawl around her shoulders.

"You keep it, then," Aunt Carrie nodded, her voice filled with compassion. "I'll just wrap your mother's ring and brooch in one of these handkerchiefs and take them home with me. I'll take good care of them so you will have them when you're older."

You think The Man will get them, don't you? Josh thought. You don't like him either.

"Would you like to come with us when we go back to Rochester tomorrow, Mattie?" Aunt Carrie asked, stroking Mattie's dark curls.

Mattie smiled and nodded. "Can Josh and Jere come, too?"

"We'll have to see what your stepfather says," Aunt Carrie said hesitantly. "Uncle can talk to him."

"Do you think he'll say we can go?" Mattie asked Josh eagerly.

"I don't know," Josh mumbled. No, he told himself.

Aunt Carrie wrapped up some flowery china cups and saucers and put them into the trunk. "So your stepfather doesn't use them for drinking his whiskey," she fretted.

"He doesn't drink out of a cup," Mattie told her seriously. "He says he hates those thin little things."

"He drinks straight out of the jug," Josh said loudly. Mattie giggled.

"I know he does, darlings," Aunt Carrie sighed, shaking her head.

Jere and his uncle stomped across the porch and hurried inside, shutting the door quickly to keep out the cold air.

"The Man's down by the river with his jug," Jere snickered, rolling his eyes and staggering around the room.

"Tsk, tsk," Aunt Carrie clucked. Turning to Uncle, she took his arm firmly. "We need to go out on the porch and talk. I don't think we should leave . . . ," she whispered, leading him outside.

When they returned a few minutes later, Uncle said, a little hesitantly, "Your Aunt Carrie would like . . . we would like you children to come and stay with us in Rochester."

"You boys can help Uncle in the store," Aunt Carrie continued cheerfully. "He's always saying he can't find anyone to work for him now that all the young men are going off to war."

"Eighteen sixty-one wasn't a good year for my dry-goods business, with the war in full swing, and 1862 isn't starting off any better." Uncle shook his head and hooked his thumbs through his suspenders, snapping them against his round belly.

Josh watched, fascinated. His suspenders didn't stretch like that. They just held up his hand-me-down pants, the ones Jere had outgrown.

"What about the war, sir?" Jere asked.

"Well, the cotton and most of the wool are going for uniforms these days. I haven't had a new shipment of calico in—"

Jere interrupted impatiently, "But how is *the war* going? Where's the fighting?"

"Our brave lads are fighting all over the south, Jeremiah. In Virginia and South Carolina, Tennessee, even on the Mississippi River."

"Nooooo! Who's winning?"

"Well, we're having some rough times right now. The army can't recruit men fast enough to keep up with the casualties. There's talk of lowering the recruitment age to sixteen."

"I'm almost fifteen."

"Yes, yes, Joshua told me. Do you know I've lost three clerks this month to that fat sergeant at the recruiting depot?"

Aunt Carrie chimed in. "He fills their heads with talk of glory and

5

offers them thirteen dollars a month, plus a bonus! We can't pay wages like that."

"Maybe I should join the army," Jere announced.

"What do you mean?" Aunt Carrie gasped.

"Maybe I should join up with that old army recruiter," Jere went on, sounding more determined, "and get thirteen dollars a month and a bonus."

Aunt Carrie stared at him, speechless for once.

"They wouldn't take you, boy," his uncle chuckled. "You're too young. There's no way you could sneak by until you're at least sixteen. Too bad, though."

"Maybe I'll just try anyway. Everyone says I'm big for my age," Jere argued.

His uncle laughed heartily. "Maybe you should try, at that. The army needs big, strong lads like you. I was just telling Joshua that you're quite a man for fourteen."

"I'll be fifteen next month. Do you really? . . ."

"*Stop that!*" Aunt Carrie cried in an anguished voice. "Stop talking that way, both of you! What would your mother say, Jeremiah. And she just now laid to rest in her grave."

"We were just fooling," Uncle said sheepishly, winking at Jere. Jere grinned.

You're not fooling, are you? Josh thought. You're serious. Oh, Jere! Don't you go, too, and leave me all alone with The Man. If you go to war and Mattie goes to Rochester, what will *I* do?

Ignoring Jere and Uncle, Aunt Carrie continued, "If you come to live with us in Rochester, you can go to school. You know, your mother was a teacher before she married your father. She would have wanted you to go to school so you could learn to read and write."

"We already know how to read and write," Mattie informed her in a superior tone. "Mother taught us how. She let us read the books she had when she was teaching and taught us arithmetic, and we read aloud from the Bible every night."

"I know she schooled you at home, dear, but in Rochester you could—"

"And she made me keep a diary and copy Bible verses in it . . . and helpful suggestions for keeping the house clean . . . and recipes." Mattie paused. "Jere is better at arithmetic than Josh and I are."

"Uncle can help you with your sums, Mattie, and I'll tell you some of my best recipes for you to copy in your diary. And poetry.

You can copy down some little poems from Charles and Mary Lamb's new book." Aunt Carrie smoothed Mattie's hair back from her forehead. "We can do all that when you come to live with me."

Suddenly, The Man's heavy boots sounded on the porch. He burst in the door, exclaiming, "Dang but it's getting cold!" Banging into a chair and knocking it over, he wove unsteadily across to the fireplace, splattering river mud from his boots onto the polished oak floor.

Aunt Carrie tsk-tsked disapprovingly and moved quickly to wipe up the mud while Josh set the chair upright.

Uncle went to The Man, speaking gently. "Carrie and I know that it will be hard for you now, without Helen."

The Man hunched his shoulders up around his thick neck as though to shield himself from Uncle's words. "We'll get by," he grunted.

"Well, we thought it might be easier for you without the children," Uncle continued.

The Man raised his head and looked at Uncle with red-rimmed eyes. He thrust his unshaven chin forward, stopping just inches from Uncle's face. Several seconds passed, half a minute.

When The Man did not say anything, Uncle tried again. "Carrie and I can take them with us to Rochester."

"You can take the girl," The Man said. "I don't need her; she's too young to be much help, but I need the boys to work the farm."

"Well, we were thinking, if we took all of them, we could bring the boys back later in the spring to help with—"

"No."

"But we—"

"No!" The Man thundered, drawing himself up, making himself look huge. "And that's final!"

"Mattie, then," Aunt Carrie pleaded. "You said we could take Mattie."

"She can go," The Man agreed.

"No!" Mattie burst out. "I won't go if Josh and Jere can't."

"But, darling, you don't want to stay out here without your mother or any other woman nearby. It's just not a good idea," Aunt Carrie coaxed.

"No," Mattie repeated. "Not if Josh and Jere can't go."

"Talk to her Josh. Tell her to come with us," Aunt Carrie begged.

"You should go, Mattie. You can go to school and—" Josh began.

"No," Mattie declared, stubborn now.

"You'll have your own room, and you can—"

"No! I'm not going without my brothers." Mattie glared defiantly at Josh and then Aunt Carrie and finally at The Man.

"That's it, then," The Man decided. "She stays."

"But . . . but . . . ," Aunt Carrie faltered.

"No more about it. They're my responsibility now, and I say they stay here. That's final!" He spoke loudly, leaving an awkward silence when he finished.

After a while, he continued in a more civil tone, "What does she need to go to school for? She can learn all she needs to know here— darning socks and skinning squirrels, making biscuits. She already knows how to tend the kitchen garden, and she's a passable cook. I don't know why I said she could go. We do need her. She stays."

Relief flooded through Josh, but as fast as it came, he pushed it away. You know she ought to go, he told himself. Be a man. Stand up to him. Tell him to let her go. He took a breath and waited.

Mattie moved with a swish of self-satisfaction and sat down next to Josh by the fire.

"Look, Mattie, you . . . ," Josh whispered.

"I'm staying here with you and Jere," she frowned, imitating her stepfather, "and that's final!"

★★ *Two* ★★

THE TREASURE

S HE stays," The Man repeated, laughing unpleasantly. He went into the small bedroom that had been walled off in one corner of the big room and came out with a bulky wool blanket. "I'll sleep in the barn tonight. You take the bed," he nodded to Aunt Carrie and Uncle. "You'll be going tomorrow?" The question sounded like an order. Uncle nodded.

Cold air rushed in when The Man went out, leaving the door ajar. His boots crunched on the cold ground as he went around the side of the house to the barn. Josh went to close the door and saw that there was still a tinge of pink on the horizon where the sun had set. A sliver of new moon slit the evening sky.

"Hurry and shut the door!" Jere called to him. Josh pulled the heavy door shut slowly, making the hinges creak loudly.

"Don't do that!" Mattie squealed.

"He's gone back to his whiskey jug, no doubt!" Aunt Carrie clucked, disapprovingly.

"Now, Carrie, he's just lost his wife and faces the responsibility of three children. He may need a sip of something to help him get along," Uncle tried to soothe her.

"He's already had quite a few sips," Jere smirked, staggering around in a circle.

"No more smart talk, Jeremiah," Aunt Carrie warned him. "You have to think of your sister now. You never can tell what someone will do when they've had too much to drink."

"Aw, he never hits too hard," Jere bragged, "and his aim isn't very good when he's 'likkered' up."

"If you just wouldn't sass him and get him riled," Josh suggested. "He gets mad at all of us when you do." He's mean, and I hate him, he thought to himself. I hate all the meanness and fighting. He and Jere seem to enjoy it.

"I'll be good," Jere grinned. "I won't make him get mad at us."

"Good lads," Uncle said, smiling at both boys.

The next morning for breakfast, Aunt Carrie fried up some ham and made little cornmeal pancakes, which they soaked in molasses. Then she and Uncle packed their satchel, and the boys hitched up the horse and buggy.

Mattie would not change her mind and go with them, so Uncle handed Aunt Carrie into the buggy. "You boys take care of your sister," Aunt Carrie cautioned them. Then she and Uncle drove sadly away, turning north along the river road toward Rochester.

The dust had hardly settled when The Man announced that he was going down river "on business." Jere snickered and winked at Josh.

"I might be back by suppertime or I might not," The Man said. "See you keep busy. Jeremiah, you and Joshua turn the hay in the stalls and then get the harrow cleaned up. Mattie, you clean out the root cellar, throw away anything that's rotten, and put some clean straw down there."

Poking at the food still on the table, he said, "Looks like there's plenty to eat, so you won't need to do any cooking for a while." He wrapped some turkey and a big piece of ham in his handkerchief and stuffed it into his woolly coat pocket along with a handful of biscuits. Taking the musket down from where it hung over the fireplace, he swaggered to the door.

"Stay out of mischief, you three!" he called over his shoulder.

He went to the barn to saddle the horse and rode away, followed by his brown mutt, Ralph. They trotted down the lane to the river road and turned south while the children stood on the porch watching.

"What kind of mischief can we get into?" Mattie giggled.

Jere climbed up on the porch rail and, holding on to a post, he leaned far out, shouting, "Good-bye. Good-bye, you old drunk, you . . ."

Josh grabbed his ankles to keep him from falling. "Shush," he warned, giving him a shake. "You heard what Uncle said about The Man. He has a lot of responsibility now, taking care of us."

"Nonsense!" Jere snorted. "He's not like that because he's taking care of us. He's been sipping from the jug for a long time." He jumped down from the railing and ran into the house, trying to slam the door so Mattie and Josh couldn't get in, but they were too quick for him. With both of them shoving, they were able to push the heavy door just enough to let Josh get halfway in. Suddenly Jere jumped aside, letting the door rush open. Into the room tumbled Mattie and Josh. Whooping, they chased Jere around and around the table, finally trapping him between them. Leaping on him, they pummeled him until he apologized.

"How good it is to have *him* gone," Mattie sighed, the end of a laugh in her voice. Then she sighed, "Oh," and tears filled her eyes, sliding down her cheeks to cling for a moment on her chin.

"Come on, Mattie, don't cry," Josh coaxed. Her tears made him feel lonely when, just a few minutes before, they had all been playing happily.

"Come on," he repeated, kneeling on the braided rug beside the old cedar chest. "Let's see what else is in here." He opened the chest, releasing the strong, clean smell of the forest.

"Here, Mattie, hold Mother's shawl." Mattie took the shawl and wrapped it around her shoulders, tucking in the ends the way her mother always used to do.

"Come on, Jere, we might find something exciting in here."

"Like what? A treasure?" Jere scoffed, but he squatted down next to Josh.

They took out the cups and saucers Aunt Carrie had put away and laid them carefully on the hearth. Underneath was a parcel wrapped in crinkly paper, the white tablecloth their mother used for Christmas dinner and birthdays.

Below that was half a bolt of blue-sprigged calico, folded neatly. Mattie's mother had made herself and Mattie dresses from the material last summer, before she became so ill. Mattie had made her rag doll a dress to match, trying to copy her mother's fine stitches.

Mattie laid the calico on the tablecloth and removed a quilt of many colors. There was a faded-red velvet heart in the center, and the names Helen and Hugh were embroidered on the heart in little white stitches. They spread the quilt on the rug and studied it for a while before turning back to the chest.

Mattie pulled out a small package tied up with blue velvet ribbon. Inside was a little dress.

"My doll could wear that," Mattie cried, holding up the lace-trimmed dress.

"That's yours," Josh laughed, pointing his finger at Mattie. "That's your baby dress. I remember."

"Yours, too," Jere crowed, pointing his finger at Josh. "You wore it when you were baptized. I remember *that*."

In the same package with the lace dress they found three baby pictures in a carved, folding frame. Each baby wore the same white lace dress.

"You, too," Mattie and Josh cried, poking their fingers at Jere.

"You were a lovely little girl," Mattie giggled.

There was a scratchy wool blanket with a frayed border and a heavy, knit sweater. In the very bottom, next to a bundle of neatly patched sheets, was a worn, brown knapsack with leather shoulder straps.

"Do you think it was Dad's?" Josh asked, pulling the knapsack out.

"Probably," Jere agreed. "Hurry up and open it."

Josh undid the tarnished brass clasp and shook the contents onto the floor. "A knife," he shouted, pushing in front of Jere to grab a sturdy pocketknife with a tortoiseshell handle.

Jere glowered at him and then snatched up a pocket watch in an elegantly engraved case that had a gold chain attached to a little loop at the top. He pried the clasp with his fingernail, and the watch case popped open. He wound the stem. In a minute, the long, black hand moved one jerk forward. Another minute, another jerk.

"It works!" he shouted, jumping up. Tucking the watch into one shirt pocket, he draped the gold chain across his stomach and tucked the other end into the side pocket of his wool pants. Brushing his hair out of his eyes, he strode importantly around the room.

"You look just like Uncle, with your belly stuck out like that," Josh teased.

Jere stuck his stomach out farther. "Get those bolts of calico down from the shelf, Joshua," he ordered. "Then see what Mrs. Fritzy over there in millinery wants." Josh laughed and Mattie clapped her hands at the performance.

"Look here," Mattie said, holding up another carved picture case. "Look," she repeated breathlessly, opening the case. Inside, the gold-edged frame held a picture of a young woman whose hair lay in dark curls around her face. A gentle smile tugged up the corners of her mouth, and her merry eyes laughed at them from the picture.

"Mother," Jere spoke quietly.

"She looks so young and happy," Mattie sighed. "I don't remember her ever looking that way."

Josh stared at the picture, trying to remember. For just a second he saw the smiling face, but then it was gone. He took the picture case from Mattie and laid it on the quilt.

An oiled canvas pouch remained on the floor, its drawstring pulled tight. Josh picked it up. Turning it upside down, he shook, spilling a torrent of gold coins out on the hard wooden floor, where they bounced and rolled, glittering, in all directions. He snatched one that rolled close to him. Jere picked up another, and another.

"The treasure," Mattie whispered, reaching for one of the coins. The boys looked at her, then at each other, their mouths gaping.

"What are they?" she demanded, holding up the coin.

Jere studied his. "Twenty dollars," he whispered hoarsely.

"Each?" Josh gasped.

"How many are there?" Mattie asked.

Jere spread the coins on the floor, moving them with his finger, counting, "One, two, three . . . nineteen—"

"Twenty," Mattie finished, adding hers to the pile.

"Whew! Four hundred dollars!" Jere whistled. "Gold!"

"Where do you think they came from?" Josh asked.

"Who put them there?" Mattie wanted to know

When Jere didn't answer, Josh persisted, "Whose are they?"

"I don't know where they came from or who put them there, but they're ours," Jere proclaimed. "*Ours!*" he shouted, leaping up and whirling around the room in a wild dance.

Josh fingered the pouch. "There's something else in here." He stuck one finger into the pouch and felt around.

"You're a slowpoke," Jere cried, snatching the pouch away from Josh and pulling out a thick piece of yellowish parchment, folded tightly.

"A treasure map!" Mattie cried.

Jere spread the paper on the floor, and they all studied it while Jere read aloud.

By Act of Congress providing for
Grants of Land in the Western Territories

Know ye that Hugh M. Parish, of Monroe County in
the State of New York, has received a grant of

Ninety-Three (93) Acres of the southwest quarter of
Section Thirty-Five, lying south of the Sweetwater
River in the Western Territory known as Wyoming.
This land is granted to Hugh M. Parish and his Heirs
forever.
By the President of the United States of America,
Franklin Pierce
Under the Seal of the Commissioner of Lands
This Twentieth day of June, 1853.

Josh peered at the yellowed paper. "Does that mean we own land, too?"

"What land?" Mattie wanted to know.

"Ninety-three acres of land someplace called Wyoming."

"Where is Wyoming?"

"What's a section of land?"

"It has Dad's name on it," Jere studied the paper, "and it says his heirs forever."

"His heirs. Is that us?" Josh asked.

"I guess it is. I guess it's our land now."

"What if The Man finds it?" Mattie breathed sharply. The boys looked at her, stricken.

"What if he finds the *money?*" Josh asked anxiously. He got up and hurried to the door, looking toward the river. "I can't see him coming."

Jere scooped up the coins and stuffed them back into the pouch, pushing the deed in, too. "We've got to hide it."

"Where?" they all said at the same time.

Looking around the room, Jere shook his head. "Not in here. He might find it."

"Where?" Mattie repeated.

"How about the barn," Josh suggested, "up in the loft."

"He never goes up there," Mattie agreed.

"Too much of a climb for him," Jere grinned.

Quickly, they stuffed the pouch and the knife and the watch back into the knapsack.

"Here," Mattie handed Jere the picture of their mother. "Put this in, too, and Mother's shawl," she added, taking off the shawl and stuffing it into the knapsack.

"Come on, Mattie. We can't put everything in," Jere complained.

14

"It was Mother's," Mattie insisted.

"It's all right. The shawl will fit," Josh decided.

Jere led the way to the barn with Josh following along, carrying the knapsack, and Mattie behind, turning to look toward the river every few steps.

"You stay here by the door and watch for him," Jere told Mattie when they reached the barn door.

"I want to come in, too, and see where you hide it," Mattie demanded.

"We'd better hurry," Josh warned. "We still have to turn the hay in the stalls before he gets back." Jere climbed the narrow ladder into the loft. Josh tossed him the knapsack and climbed up, pulling Mattie along behind him. He opened the loft door so she could look west toward the river.

"Here, Mattie, you can see where we hide the knapsack and watch the river at the same time." Mattie squinted into the afternoon sun.

"I see something," she squealed. "I think it's him. Oh, what are we going to do?" Josh and Jere scrambled to the farthest, darkest corner of the loft, scraped back handfuls of loose hay, and buried the knapsack. They piled hay back on top. Then they all tumbled down the ladder. Grabbing a pitchfork, Jere raced for the stalls. Trembling, Josh followed. They dug furiously in the matted hay on the floor. Mattie ran to get an armload of fresh hay and stumbled toward Josh and Jere.

"What are you doing in here?" The Man's voice thundered from the door.

Mattie froze, speechless, hugging the prickly hay.

"She's helping us," Jere answered, swaggering from the stall. Soiled hay clung to the legs of his pants; some stuck in his hair.

"You look like you've been rolling in it," The Man sneered with disgust. "Be sure you clean up before you come in the house."

"Yes, sir."

Josh slipped out of the stall to stand a little behind Jere. Peering at The Man, he asked cautiously, "Are you going out again? Would you like me to take care of the horse for you, sir?"

"I decided not to go down river today. You can unsaddle the horse." He turned on his heel and went to the house.

"Ssst, Josh! Jere! Come here!" Mattie hissed from the corner of the barn. "Look!"

15

"What is it?"

She pointed proudly to a dozen crockery whiskey jugs she had uncovered from beneath a pile of hay.

"Whew," Jere whistled.

"So that's where he keeps 'em," Josh said.

"What are we going to do with them?" Mattie wanted to know.

"Nothing now," Jere decided.

"We could break them," Mattie suggested hopefully.

"Not now, Mattie. What good would it do?" Jere asked.

Disappointment crumpled Mattie's face.

"Cover them up," Jere ordered.

Mattie and Josh piled hay back on top of the jugs. Then they finished their chores and went to the pump to wash up.

"I wish we could have smashed them," Mattie sighed, wistfully.

"We will someday," Jere promised.

✭✭ *Three* ✭✭

GOOSY

I N the following weeks, neighbors stopped by to see how the family was getting on. They brought pie or a slab of bacon and talked about the weather and the crops and the war.

"Those Johnny Rebs are whupping us down there," young Mr. Hobbs reported, handing Mattie some pickles his wife had sent along. "The casualty list in Geneseo gets longer every week."

"Where's the war? Where are they fighting?" Jere asked eagerly when the preacher came to call.

"Everywhere, it seems. Ever since Bull Run, our boys have been losing ground in Virginia," the preacher answered. He set a loaf of freshly baked brown bread on the kitchen table. "My son writes very discouraging letters from the Shenandoah Valley. They march up and down the valley and can never catch that General Jackson."

Late at night, Jere whispered to Josh. "Wouldn't it be glorious to see soldiers marching up and down this valley. The cannon going *bam! bam!* and the muskets answering *crash! crash!* and all the—"

"Shush!" Josh interrupted. "You'll wake him up."

"Pshaw, little brother, just listen to him snore. He won't wake up until morning."

After a few warm days in early April, wildflowers burst into splashes of purple and yellow in the fields and against the dark trees of the woods. The poplars along the river budded out with tiny, light-green leaves so bright they hurt the eyes.

Mattie swept under the beds and behind the dresser. She hung blankets and mattresses over the porch railing and beat them with a broom handle. Crawling down into the still-cold root cellar, she cleaned out shriveled, rotting vegetables, saving a basket of soft red apples that were still good enough to cook. Only a few potatoes remained, and they would be gone soon. The new crop would not be ready for many weeks, so they would have to make do with turnips.

Josh and Jere cleared the cornfields of stubble left from the fall harvest. They hitched the horse to the harrow and pulled its long rakelike fingers through the clods of earth, breaking them into small pieces that they then attacked with hoes. After many days, the soil was ready for planting.

The children's favorite job was repairing the scarecrow that would guard the cornfields from hungry crows all summer. In the evening, Mattie sat in her mother's rocker by the fireplace and mended the scarecrow's tattered shirt with patches of the blue-sprigged calico from the old chest. Jere stuffed him with fresh straw, shoving some down Josh's back, too. When they were finished, Josh crowned the scarecrow with his outgrown straw hat. They fixed the handsome fellow onto a pole and drove the pointed end into the earth in the field near the pond.

The Man sharpened the knives and hoes, and mended the big leather harness for the horse. He asked Mattie to write him out a list of what was needed from the general store in Geneseo.

"You want me to bring you some cloth for a new dress?" he asked. "You're about to burst the seams of that one," he grinned, looking Mattie up and down, reaching out to touch her.

"No," Mattie answered, turning quickly away. "There's material in the cedar chest."

Josh hitched the horse and wagon and brought it from the barn. The Man climbed up on the rough, wooden seat and whistled to Ralph who had been napping under the porch.

"I'll leave you boys the musket. You might get a wild goose or a pheasant if you keep your eyes open. Hang it down in the smokehouse till I get back. Should be two, three days at the most."

"Will you bring back a newspaper, sir?" Jere asked politely.

"Why? So you can fill your head with war nonsense!" The Man grumbled. Without giving Josh an answer, he drove away with Ralph trotting behind.

When he had gone, Jere took down the musket. "I didn't think he'd leave it." He strutted around the room with the gun on his shoulder. "Come on, Josh, let's go and get ourselves some Johnny Rebs."

"Squirrel or rabbit would taste better," Josh answered.

Jere carried the musket most of the afternoon, marching, ducking behind trees, dropping down on his stomach to take aim at a bush or a rock. Finally Josh talked Jere into letting him carry the gun for a while and nailed a gray squirrel that had stood flicking its tail beside a hickory tree.

Mattie roasted the squirrel with the last potatoes. She steamed some of the withered apples and covered them with the cow's fresh cream.

"Good food, Mattie," Jere imitated The Man, wiping his mouth on his shirt sleeve and patting his full stomach.

Josh pretended to snap his plain cotton suspenders.

"Yours don't stretch like Uncle's," Jere laughed at him.

"Well, they hold my pants up just as well," Josh shot back.

"*My* pants, you mean. You didn't get them until I outgrew 'em."

"So? You wore all the itch out of them for me," he told Jere with a grin. He thought to himself, "If you only knew how comfortable your hand-me-down's are. Softer than the new ones you get." All the same, he wished sometimes that he were a little bigger so he didn't have to wear suspenders or tie a rope around the waist to make Jere's clothes fit.

They talked until the fire was low in the hearth. Then Josh finished the evening with a Bible verse.

In the middle of the night, Josh was awakened by a rustling sound. As he held his breath and listened, it came, closer, closer. Something in the grass. Now he could hear small noises, like someone whimpering.

He sat up and looked around the darkened room. Jere snored softly in the bed next to him. On her trundle bed, Mattie stirred and reached for her rag doll, pulling it under the blanket with her.

Josh climbed out of bed and tiptoed to the door, opening it slowly so it wouldn't creak. He peered into the chilly blackness outside.

Suddenly Mattie was beside him whispering, "What is it? What's there?"

"I'm not sure. Listen."

The rustling had stopped and they heard a comfortable sound, like people talking far away.

"The geese are back," Jere grumbled loudly from the bed. "Now close the door and get into bed. I'm freezing!"

Slamming the door, Josh and Mattie scurried across the room and jumped into their beds.

"Brrr!" Josh burrowed deep into the blanket, pulling it away from Jere.

"Gimme that," Jere bellowed.

"No, you have it all. Give me some."

"*You're* taking it all," Jere complained.

"I'm freezing, too," Mattie wailed. "Can I crawl in with you?" Without waiting for an answer, she scrambled in next to Josh. He moved over to make room for her.

"Yikes! Your feet are like ice. Get 'em off me!" Jere yelled. Sitting up in bed, he snatched the covers from Josh, rolled up in a ball and turned to face the wall.

Mattie and Josh pounced on him, pummeling and tickling, tearing away the blanket. Mattie smacked Jere with her small pillow.

"No fair!" Jere hooted. "Two against one. That's no fair." Soon they were all laughing and smacking each other with pillows and snatching at the blankets. It was a long time before they stopped and went to back to sleep.

In the morning, all the Canada geese were gone from the field where they had been during the night. When Mattie and Josh finished their morning chores, they wandered down to the pond and took turns on the rope swing, which hung from a broad oak branch. They twisted the rope tight and, standing on the knot at the bottom, whirled madly around and around until they were dizzy and fell into the reeds, letting the world spin around them.

Lying on the ground, Josh stretched out his arm. Suddenly, he felt a sharp, stabbing pain in his palm. He sat up, his head still spinning, and yelled.

The pain in his hand cleared his head, and he saw two beady eyes staring at him from the reeds. Just inches away, a great, gray goose struggled to his feet. He flapped one dark wing. The other wing hung, useless, by his side. His long, black neck stretched and twisted, showing a triangular patch of white feathers under his chin.

Crawling on her knees, Mattie approached. "Oh! Josh, he's beautiful," she gasped.

"Watch out, Mattie," Josh spoke sharply, putting out a warning hand. "He bit me."

Mattie shook Josh off saying, "Of course he did. You frightened him."

"Get back, Mattie." Jere, who had come running when he heard Josh scream, seized Mattie's arm. "He can hurt you."

"I'll say he can!" Josh wailed, shaking his hand.

"He won't hurt me. It's just that you've frightened him." Shaking off Jere's grip, Mattie sat down a little ways from the goose, which stretched his long neck toward her. "I won't hurt you," she murmured softly, reaching her hand out toward the goose, which watched her but did not move.

"Go get some corn," Mattie ordered between her teeth.

"Aw, come on, Mattie. The man would skin us if he knew we'd given chicken feed to a wild goose," Jere grumbled.

"Josh, please?" Mattie asked, her eyes pleading.

Avoiding Jere's glare, Josh scrambled up and hurried to the barn, coming back in a few minutes with his pockets full of corn. "That's all, I promise," he told Jere.

Mattie sprinkled a handful for the goose. As the bird picked up each kernel, Mattie moved her hand forward slowly until she could touch his head. Gently, she ran her fingers down his neck to the useless wing. The goose flapped the other wing wildly and Mattie scrambled back, startled.

She moved forward again. "Why didn't you go with the others?" she crooned softly.

"Maybe he's been shot," Josh said. "See, there's blood on his wing." He pointed to the thick, shoulder part of the wing where the dark feathers were matted with dried blood.

The goose struggled to his feet, wobbling as he tried to stand. One webbed foot was bloody, too, and he pulled that up, tucking it into his white breast feathers.

Josh crawled forward cautiously and knelt beside the goose. Hesitantly, he ran his hand over the injured wing. The goose quivered but did not bite him again.

"Good Goosy. Josh won't hurt you," Mattie murmured, sounding a lot like another goose.

With gentle fingers, Josh pulled the hidden leg down so he could feel it. "I don't think the foot's broken," he said, letting go. "I can't tell about the wing." He touched the wing, and the goose hissed at him and hopped away.

"Come on, Goosy, we have to find a place to keep you," Mattie coaxed, walking slowly toward the barn. The goose hopped after her on his good leg.

"You can't keep him in the barn. The Man won't let you keep him as a pet," Jere called after her.

"He might if we are *all* very nice to him when he gets home," Mattie tossed back at him.

"And if we're *all* polite," Josh said pointedly.

"The Man won't let you. You'll see," Jere warned with a shrug.

The next day, Mattie talked softly to the goose while she fed him. Soon the goose was following her around the barnyard hopping on one foot, trying to nuzzle her apron pocket where she kept the corn. When the goose was full of corn, Josh fingered the injured wing, deciding it was not broken.

"Would it help to bandage it?" Mattie asked, wanting to be helpful. "I can tear up some rags."

"I don't think he'd keep a bandage on," Josh laughed, but Mattie pleaded, so of course he tried. After that, the goose strutted around the barnyard, seeming proud of his bandaged wing.

Next to the chicken house Josh built a little enclosure where the goose could stay at night. He figured the goose would keep the raccoons from getting the little chicks while Ralph was gone.

He was working in the field when Josh saw The Man coming home. He called out the alarm to the others, then ran as fast as he could to meet The Man at the barn door. "Here, sir, let me help you with the wagon."

The Man nodded. "Thank you, boy."

Jere came tearing around the corner of the barn. "I'll help you unload, sir," he gasped, catching his breath. The Man looked from Jere to Josh, puzzled.

After the boys unhitched the horse and led him to his stall, they worked together to pull the heavy seed sacks off the wagon and carry them into the barn. The Man watched, saying nothing.

Mattie appeared around the side of the barn followed by the goose with his bandaged wing, hopping on his one good leg.

The Man laughed heartily. "What do we have here?"

"He's a Canada goose," Mattie told him sweetly "He couldn't fly away when the others left. Isn't he beautiful?"

"Looks crippled to me," The Man said bluntly.

"Josh has been taking care of him and he's almost well," Mattie gulped, trying to smile. "He follows me everywhere I go. May I keep him, please?"

The Man looked from Josh to Jere, then back to Mattie and the goose. "Sure. Why not?" he shrugged. "It'll be a good Christmas dinner." Turning on his heel, he stalked toward the house.

At dinner, Mattie's furious eyes burned into The Man as she slammed his plate down in front of him. "Watch it, girl," he growled, slapping at her, but she slipped quickly out of his reach.

"Here, sir, let me get you some coffee." Josh stood up, putting himself between Mattie and The Man. He mustn't let The Man hit her. Trembling, he held the back of the chair to steady himself.

The Man bent his head over his plate and continued to eat, leaning back in his chair when he had finished.

"Your Yankee army isn't doing very well," he baited Jere.

"That so?" Jere was interested in spite of himself. "Did you hear that in town?"

"I did."

"Did you bring a paper?"

"No need to waste money on a paper. The war's all people talked about. To hear some people talk, you'd think it was every man's duty to enlist and march off and get himself killed."

"When are you going?" Mattie asked with forced sweetness in her voice.

"I'm not. Why should I get myself killed in Mr. Lincoln's war?"

When no one answered, The Man stood up and headed for the door. "Going to check on things in the barn," he said over his shoulder. Mattie cringed in disgust as bits of biscuit fell from his unkempt beard.

When he was gone, Jere rolled his eyes and staggered around the table. "Sure he's going to check on things. He's checking on his whiskey jugs."

"*Stop it, Jere!* This is no time for joking," Mattie fumed. "We have to do something or he'll kill Goosy for Christmas dinner."

"Aw, Mattie, maybe he was just teasing," Jere tried to soothe her.

"It wasn't funny," Mattie snapped.

"He wasn't just teasing," Josh said. "We have to make a plan."

"To save a goose?" Jere asked. "We have to make a plan to save a goose?"

"Just pretend it's the war," Josh coaxed. "You're good at planning, Jere. Help us."

Reluctant at first, Jere finally agreed. "All right. All right. We'll think of a battle plan. That old drunk will never get one bite of Goosy." He slapped his knee and grinned at Mattie and Josh.

Although they all suggested many ideas, they could not decide on one they agreed would work. At last Mattie decided they would teach the goose to fly all over again. "When his wing gets stronger," she added.

"The perfect plan!" Jere laughed. "Now all we have to do is teach a silly goose how to fly."

"If we can just get him off the ground, he'll probably go with the other geese when they come back in October," Josh told them.

Mattie's face fell. "What if he won't go? What if he won't fly away?"

"Like you," Josh said. "Like you wouldn't go to Rochester with Aunt Carrie when you had the chance."

Mattie stuck her tongue out at him and flounced outside into the twilight, scaring the goose so it flapped its wings and hopped around in a circle, honking.

They worked hard during the long summer days, but the work was not unpleasant because they could see the corn growing taller. The squash and bean plants flowered and produced vegetables. At the end of the day, the children raced to the pond, stripping their clothes off as they went. Josh and Jere climbed the tree and crawled out on the big branch which spread over the pond. They pulled the heavy rope up and jumped off the branch, swinging way out over the pond and splashing into the cool water, which bubbled up from a spring deep in the ground.

More modest than her brothers, Mattie gathered her petticoats around her and waded into the water until air filled the undergarments and buoyed her up so she could float.

One day as they emerged dripping and muddy, The Man was standing behind the tree watching them. "You're too big to act like that," he scolded. After that they only swam in the pond when he was gone.

Each time he went away, they tried to get the goose to fly. The first time, Jere held him up off the ground and let him drop in a heap. Fluttering up onto one leg, the goose flapped and honked around the barnyard after Jere who danced away and finally clambered over a rail fence to safety. Josh rolled in the dust, laughing, while Mattie soothed the ruffled goose.

After that, the boys let Mattie do the dropping. They helped her climb the loft ladder, just a little ways at first. Then they handed the goose up to her. She murmured softly, telling the goose that he had to fly and how to flap his wings. "Remember. Remember," she whispered. "You remember how to do it." Then she dropped him onto a pile of straw at the base of the ladder.

After a while the goose began to flap his wings and honk when Mattie dropped him, flying around inside the barn before coming to rest at her feet.

In August, they hauled him up into the barn loft, huffing and gasping because the goose had grown fat from all the corn. They dropped him out of the high loft door. The goose never faltered. He flew in a great circle around the farm swooping and gliding, then rising and soaring over the fields. Finally he landed in the barnyard where they had run to watch. He nuzzled in Mattie's pocket for corn.

"What if he won't go away in October?" Mattie fretted.

"He'll go," Josh assured her, hoping he was right.

Neighbors came to help with the harvest in September, and the men talked about the war. There had been a second disaster for the Union Army at Bull Run in Virginia.

"The Rebs call it Manassas down there," young Mr. Hobbs explained to Jere. "That's the name of the town nearby. Casualties are so high now that there's not many who will sign up for a second enlistment when their first is up."

"Thirteen dollars a month, even with a bonus, is not worth being shot at, maybe killed," the preacher's son told them.

Despite the discouraging news, Jere continued to talk about going off to war. When he hunted, he marched through the woods whooping, "Got you, Johnny Reb!"

The Canada geese returned one October evening just as a round yellow moon rose above the trees. They circled the farm before settling down in the harvested fields beside the pond. The children heard them honking and rustling in the stubble all night.

Long before daylight, they crept noiselessly from their beds and dressed. When they went outside, Goosy came from his coop and followed Mattie, nuzzling hungrily in her pocket.

"Stop that!" Mattie burst out. "You're not a pet. Get away." She shooed and flapped her skirt at the goose. She tried to chase him toward the cornfield, but he just ran around behind her and tried to reach her pocket again.

"Go away!" Mattie cried. "You've got to go away!"

"If we chase the other geese and get them to fly away, maybe our goose will follow," Josh suggested.

They climbed into the loft in the barn, hauling the goose behind them up the ladder. "You stay here by the loft door while Josh and I go down and chase the others away," Jere told Mattie. "When they start flying, push Goosy out."

"Can you do that? Can you make him fly away?" Josh asked.

Mattie nodded and turned away from him to stand with the goose by the open door. As the sky lightened, Josh and Jere ran into the field by the pond, waving their arms and shouting at the geese there. Startled at first, the geese ran around in circles, flapping their wings, honking, hissing, and snapping at the boys. Then, with great dignity, they spread their wings, ran several steps and took off into the dawn.

As the geese flew overhead, Mattie shoved Goosy out of the high door. "Go!" she sobbed. "Go away. Don't ever come back again. Please!" She scrambled down the ladder and ran out into the barnyard to stand with her brothers.

Goosy circled the farm with the other geese as the flock flew higher and higher. Slowly they all formed a V behind their leader and disappeared over the southern horizon.

★★ *Four* ★★

THIN ICE

WINTER was coming. Josh and Mattie shucked corn and filled the corncrib in the barn. The sharp edges of the husks cut their hands and the prickly hairs scratched their skin. They longed to bathe in the farm pond, but it was too cold now. Jere helped The Man prepare the harvested fields, pushing the plow blade deep into the earth to break the soil into large chunks that would be harrowed in the spring.

Mattie dug up all the potatoes from the garden because the ground would freeze soon. She laid them on the cool earth floor of the root cellar beneath the house. Then she filled baskets with turnips and cabbages, and apples from the orchard, packing straw all around to protect them from the cold. She tied herbs into bunches and braided onions to hang from the rafters in the kitchen.

Jere and Josh helped Mr. Hobbs butcher his hogs and came home with half of one, which they hung in the smokehouse to cure. They were all so busy that they hardly realized when November passed into December. Then it snowed, and the fields were blanketed in white and the pond froze solid—except in the very middle, where the spring bubbled up. The ice was thin there.

Aunt Carrie and Uncle arrived on Christmas Eve in a sled loaded with gifts and a fat turkey and good cheer. In just one afternoon, they transformed the bleak farmhouse into a cheery home, with hugs and kisses and paper garlands strung everywhere. The smell of cinnamon and other spices filled the room.

The men went into the forest to cut a tree, with Uncle puffing behind as they tramped through the knee-deep snow. When they came back, they could hardly drag the huge tree through the door and had to saw six inches off the bottom so the top didn't bend over where it touched the rafters. Now the clean smell of pine mixed with the odor of spices. In the evening, all of them— even The Man—sang Christmas songs, while Mattie and Aunt Carrie strung berries and popped corn for the tree.

All morning on Christmas Day, Aunt Carrie stood by the warm oven basting a fat, brown turkey. Every time she opened the oven door, Josh thought he would die from hunger. With a fork, he poked a piece of bread into the rich brown juices in the bottom of the pan. Aunt Carrie shooed him away, and Jere snatched the dripping bread and ate it, burning his mouth. They all hooted as Jere whirled around the room, howling and laughing. The Man came in from the barn. His eyes were red from the cold, and he had snowflakes sticking to his face and clothes.

"I could smell that bird all the way to the barn," he murmured pleasantly.

Aunt Carrie beamed. "Dinner's almost ready. Jere, you clear those things off your stepfather's chair and make a place for him to sit down. Mattie, you and Josh get the tablecloth out of the cedar chest and spread it on the table."

"Yes, Ma'am." They moved quickly to do what they were told.

Uncle said a prayer before they ate, remembering the children's parents and asking God's blessing on their little family. He prayed for soldiers they knew fighting in the war on this holiday. He prayed for President Lincoln and for peace. Finally, they all said, "Amen."

They filled their plates with turkey and cornbread stuffing, sweet potatoes and mashed potatoes and gravy. When they had eaten all they could, Aunt Carrie set out mince pie and apple pie, cheese and coffee. She enjoyed cooking, as her ample figure showed.

"Fine meal, Carrie," The Man said, pushing himself back from the table and patting his full stomach. The children giggled.

"I'm glad you enjoyed it," Aunt Carrie answered, fluttering around the table, cleaning up.

Uncle took out the newspaper he had brought. "Sad news from the war, Jeremiah. A bad defeat for our boys at Fredericksburg. Now both armies are in camp for the winter. Here, you may have the paper. I know you like to read about it yourself." He handed the folded paper to Jere.

"No talk of war today." The Man snatched the paper from Jere and threw it into the fire. "Let's not talk of war after such a fine meal."

"Why'd you do that?" Jere cried, jumping up, knocking over his chair. "It's burning up." He ran toward the fireplace, but The Man stopped him.

"Let it burn, Jeremiah," he warned. "Why do you want to fill your mind with all that war nonsense?"

Jere turned away, angry, muttering under his breath.

"What did you say?" The Man fumed, his good humor gone.

Jere stalked sullenly toward the door, but his uncle reached it first. "Go back and sit down, young man," he spoke firmly to Jere. Jere looked around, wanting to get away but not wanting to shove his uncle.

Aunt Carrie swooped in. "Now let's all sit down and finish our coffee," she soothed. "Then I have a special treat." She moved here and patted there, taking The Man by the arm and bringing him back to the table. Uncle brought Jere. Josh turned Jere's chair right-side up for him and then sat back down next to Mattie and squeezed her hand gently.

"It's all right," he whispered.

"No, it's not." She snatched her hand away.

You're right, it isn't, Josh thought sadly. But we have to make it all right. Otherwise The Man and Jere will fight all through Christmas.

"Smile," he said, more to himself than to Mattie. Taking her hand again, he repeated, "It's all right," but Mattie ignored him.

"Gather 'round, all of you," Aunt Carrie directed, pulling and pushing everyone toward the tree, where there were several packages tied with red ribbon.

"Here." She handed a parcel to The Man and fussed at him until he pulled the ribbon off and opened the paper. Inside was a thick wool sweater, big and black.

To match your scowl, Josh thought.

From behind the tree where it had been hidden, Uncle dragged out a long, thin parcel wrapped in brown paper that could not disguise what was inside.

"Here, Jeremiah. This is for you."

Tearing off the paper, Jere almost exploded. "It's mine! My own musket!" he cried over and over.

"That's a useful gift," The Man said. "Now you won't be taking mine all the time."

Aunt Carrie brought Mattie a box, carefully wrapped in shiny paper and tied with blue ribbons.

"You can use these to tie up your hair," she said as she helped Mattie undo the ribbons. It was obvious that Aunt Carrie was more excited than Mattie, who still looked cross from the earlier unpleasantness.

Come on, Mattie, Josh thought. Don't be mean to Aunt Carrie. She's trying her best to make everything all right.

As though she knew what he was thinking, Mattie smiled at Aunt Carrie. She removed the lid of the box and drew out a delicate doll. The doll's dress was blue silk draped over clouds of lace petticoats. Her face and hands were china, as delicate as Mama's cups.

"Her name is Jerusha. I saw her in the window of the shop next to Uncle's and I just had to get her for you," Aunt Carrie prattled, fingering the soft dress and smoothing the doll's golden curls. "You'll have to take very good care so that her face and fingers don't chip."

Josh wondered where Mattie could keep the doll that it wouldn't get broken. "Maybe on the mantel," he said.

"What? What did you say?" Mattie asked sharply.

"I said maybe you could keep the doll on the mantel," Josh repeated. Mattie nodded and carried the doll to the fireplace, propping it carefully on the mantel shelf. She thanked Aunt Carrie and kissed her and sat down quietly.

The Man sat at the table, tugging at the sweater in his lap, not smiling. Jere had gone out on the porch to aim at the barn and pretend to pull the trigger of his new musket. Uncle handed Josh a small package.

Not a musket for me, Josh thought, turning the package over and over in his hands.

"Open it," Mattie ordered.

He lingered, looking at the wrapping, turning the package. He tried to remember the last time someone had given him a present all wrapped up and tied with ribbon.

"Why don't you open it?" Mattie asked more impatiently. Josh continued to savor the package.

"For pity's sake, open it! It won't bite you," Jere taunted from the door.

Josh drew off the ribbon and folded back the paper. A grin crept across his face. Inside lay a pair of shiny black suspenders with gold buckles just like his uncle's. He pulled on the tabs and let them snap back, stinging his fingers.

"I saw you eyeing mine when I was here for . . . when we were here before. These are just like them." Uncle hovered beside him. "I ordered them from New York City, especially for you. Do you like 'em?"

"I do." Josh smiled broadly. "I really do." He gave his uncle an unexpected hug and reached for Aunt Carrie, who crushed him to her generous bosom. When she finally let him go, Josh removed his old, webbed suspenders and buttoned the new ones to his trousers.

"Makes those pants look like they fit you," Jere laughed at him. For the rest of the day, he came up behind Josh and snapped the suspenders. After a while, Josh got tired of it, but he didn't want to say anything that might spoil the day, so he just tried to keep away from Jere.

Aunt Carrie and Uncle left the next day. They tried to get Mattie to come with them, but she wouldn't.

In the first week of 1863, a blizzard raged across Lake Ontario and down the Genesee Valley. Snow blew up against the north window so they couldn't see anything outside but whiteness. When The Man went to the barn to feed the livestock, he tied one end of a rope to the porch railing, paying it out between his fingers as he went so he could find his way back. When he came in, he had a jug partially hidden under his heavy coat; everybody saw it.

By the middle of the afternoon, it was so dark they had to light candles. They kept the fire going but used logs sparingly in case it was a long storm.

Josh made up a story about wild forest animals and told it to Mattie while she darned his socks. She made him tell it again so that she could copy it into her diary, right after the recipe for molasses cookies. She formed her letters carefully so they looked as though they had been printed. Then she read the story back to Josh. He noticed that she had added names for the animals and described them carefully and even given them words to say. He liked her story better than his own, which seemed colorless by comparison.

While this was going on, Jere cleaned and oiled his musket; The Man sipped whiskey and grew bleary-eyed. He set the jug on the floor by his foot where he could reach it easily. He was still sitting by the fire when the children said their prayers and went to sleep.

The next day the wind stopped howling, and the snow stopped

swirling. The whole world outside was silent. The boys waded through the snow to the barn to give the horse oats and put fresh hay in the stall for the cow. They threw several ears of dried corn in the stall where the chickens were roosting for the winter and laid down some scraps for Ralph. Of course they didn't feed the barn cat. He had to be hungry so he would catch the mice that got into the corncrib to feast.

On the way back to the house, they stopped at the woodshed and brought back armloads of logs, making several trips. Then they dug out the slanted door to the root cellar and crawled down inside, holding a lighted candle to see where they were going. They fetched potatoes and vegetables for Mattie, in case another blizzard came.

They had eaten the last of the bread the night before, so Mattie mixed warm water and starter dough in a large, crockery bowl. Then she stirred in scoops of flour and a pinch of salt and added some lard. Finally, she kneaded until the bread dough was smooth and shiny. She put this in the warming box by the hearth.

As they waited for the dough to rise, the children took turns reading aloud from *Gulliver's Travels,* their favorite of their mother's books. After a while, The Man said crossly, "Stop that infernal chattering so I can think!"

"What about?" Jere whispered to Mattie, who giggled. Josh shushed them.

The next few days were warmer, and they could move about the farm more easily. One afternoon, as the early twilight settled, The Man took a lantern and went to the barn "to check on things." When supper was ready and The Man had not come back, Josh, who was hungry, went to see what had happened.

As he pushed open the door, he saw The Man sprawled, sound asleep and snoring, on a pile of hay. Muttering, The Man threw out his arm, knocking over the lantern which stood on the hay beside him. Immediately, the hay flared up.

Josh yanked off his coat and beat at the flames, pushing The Man aside and beating at his burning clothes.

"Jere! Mattie! Help!" he screamed as loud as he could.

They won't hear me, he thought and opened the barn door. The draft from the open door fanned the flames and he ran back inside, yelling as he went.

Awake now, The Man was able to pull off his smoking coat and beat at the flames, too. Jere and Mattie appeared in the doorway and immediately raced to bring buckets of water from the barrel stored in the corner. Within a few minutes, the fire was out and only soot and smoke and fear remained.

The Man was not badly burned, only frightened and angry. He grumbled at the children and went back to the house, leaving them to clean up the mess. When they had dragged the burned hay outside into the snow and turned the remaining good hay inside to be sure there was no fire left, they sat on the barn floor, shivering, and talked about what had almost happened.

"The whole place could have gone up in flames!" Jere waved his arms wildly and cursed The Man.

"That's not going to do any good," Josh told him. "What we need to do is figure out how we can keep it from happening again."

"How do you think we can do that? Do you want to follow him around everywhere he goes?" Jere asked, sarcastically.

"No, but we have to do something. We could take turns, watch him all the time," Josh suggested.

"You mean make a schedule? You watch him for eight hours, then it's Mattie's turn and then . . ."

"Why don't you ever take what I say seriously?"

"Because you're my little brother, that's why." Jere scoured Josh's head with his knuckles.

"But I have good ideas. You just don't listen to—"

"Be quiet!" Mattie spoke sharply. "I have something important to say!"

The brothers were so surprised by her tone that they stopped wrangling and listened.

"What about the treasure?" Mattie asked dramatically.

Her question was greeted with silence. After a long while, Jere spoke. "You're right, both of you. We have to do something. We have to protect our treasure. Let's think."

Josh and Mattie nodded.

It was too cold to stay in the barn, so they went back to the house and ate supper without talking. The Man disappeared into the alcove, and soon they could hear him snoring.

They talked for a long time before they agreed, but they decided to wait until morning when it was light to carry out their plans.

Very early, before The Man had even stirred in his bed, they dressed and went to the barn. While Mattie climbed up in the loft and dug the knapsack out from its straw hiding place, Josh and Jere shoveled away the dirt in one corner of the barn floor. When they came to the stone foundation, they used an iron bar to pry out several large stones and dug out the dirt underneath. Mattie handed them the knapsack, which they shoved way down in the ground where flames could not reach it. Then they pushed and shoved to fit the stones back where they had been.

Breathing a sigh of relief, they jumped up and began a wild dance, stamping down the dirt on the barn floor.

"What are you doing?" The Man's voice bellowed from the door.

"What are we going to do?" Mattie said in a frightened whisper as The Man came closer, peering into the dim light. "He'll see where we've buried it."

Suddenly, Jere jumped up and called out, "What's the matter? Afraid we'll find your 'woosky'?" He darted toward the pile of hay where The Man's jugs were hidden.

The Man lunged at Jere, who whirled away and fled out the open door into bright sunlight. Plunging through the snow, he led The Man, who was panting heavily now, through the blinding-white fields toward the pond. Racing past the oak tree, he gave the rope swing a whack and sent it spinning.

Laughing, he skated out onto the icy pond, whirling and twirling like a crazy top. The Man never paused as he charged out onto the ice, his heavy steps sending shivers across the glistening surface.

Near the center of the pond, Jere stopped. "Go back!" he shouted. "The ice won't hold you!"

The Man kept coming.

From the bank, Josh, who had followed them, screamed, "Stop! The ice is cracking! I can hear it!"

Jere skated easily to the opposite side of the pond, but The Man, trying to stop, slipped and fell, crashing down in the very center of the pond, where the ice was thin. It shattered, and The Man fell into the freezing water.

"Get him, Jere! He'll drown in there!" Josh shouted.

Jere did not move. "The ice is too weak now," he yelled back. "I can't get across it."

"We have to try," Josh wailed. "We can't let him drown."

"He'll freeze first," Jere said. He had come around the edge of the pond and was standing beside Josh now. Mattie ran up behind them and held on to the rope swing to steady herself.

The Man was screaming at them from the water, clawing at the ice, trying to get out. Each time he tried to heave himself up onto the ice, more ice broke and he fell back into the water. "Help!" he screamed. "Help me!"

"The rope!" Josh cried. "If we untie the rope, we can throw it to him and pull him out."

"It's too dangerous," Jere said, trying to catch Josh who was already scrambling up the tree.

"I have to try!" he called back. With freezing hands, he clawed at the knotted rope. Slowly, the knot loosened.

"Hurry! He's slipping under!" Mattie cried.

The rope came loose and fell to the snowy bank below. Josh jumped from the branch into the soft snow and grabbed the rope. Running to the edge, he began to move out across the ice toward The Man.

"Stop!" Jere yelled, grabbing Josh's arm and dragging him back off the ice. Josh tried to shake him off, but he was not strong enough.

Suddenly, with all his strength, he shoved Jere away from him into the snow. Then, whirling around in a circle, he threw the heavy rope as far out to the center of the pond as he could. It did not reach The Man.

Lying on his stomach, he squirmed forward, pushing the rope, like a giant snake, ahead of him. The ice beneath him shuddered.

"Josh!" Mattie screamed.

"Come back, little brother. Please," Jere begged.

Josh inched forward again. With a feeble effort, The Man caught hold of the knotted end of the rope and hung on as Josh slid back to shore.

Together, the three children pulled and pulled. The rope was soon covered with blood from their torn hands, but they pulled harder, wrapping the rope around the tree trunk so it would not slip back with The Man's sodden weight. They pulled him through the cracking ice and freezing water like a giant monster from the depths of the pond.

When he reached the solid ice at the edge, The Man heaved himself out onto the bank and collapsed in spasms of shivering.

"We have to get him back to the house and inside where it's warm before he freezes solid," Josh warned.

"Me, too!" Jere added. "Let's go."

Holding onto his legs, the two boys dragged The Man across the snowy field, through the barnyard, and up the bumpy stairs to the porch.

"I can walk! I can walk!" The Man kept shouting, but when he tried, he just fell down again. Jere laughed.

"I'll get you, boy!" The Man threatened through chattering teeth.

★★ *Five* ★★

ROCHESTER

JOSH lay on his belly in the snow. Pressing the cold musket barrel to his cheek, he carefully lined up the sights on something moving through the trees across the clearing. Slowly, very slowly and gently, he squeezed the trigger. A thunderous crash exploded in his ear, filling the clearing and echoing through the forest.

"Got him clean through the head," Jere yelled from behind. "Good shooting, little brother."

"Rabbit stew for supper," Josh whooped as he raced across the clearing to collect the rabbit. "Won't Mattie be pleased to have something to put in that old iron pot besides squirrel?" He sniffed the air, searching for a memory he could not quite recall, his mother smiling, the smell of fresh-made stew. Instead he breathed in the chill March air of the forest.

Snatching his musket, Jere put it on his shoulder and marched away. "I'm going to join Mr. Lincoln's army."

"You've been saying that for a year."

"This time I mean it. I'm going when The Man goes down river again."

"What's going to happen to Mattie and me if you go?"

"I've got that all figured out. When I go, I'll take you to Rochester to stay with Aunt Carrie. I've got to go soon, Josh. Can't you see that? I've got to get there before the war is over."

"Seems to me that the war's a long ways from over. I don't see why you want to go anyway. Good way to get killed," Josh grumbled.

"Not me. I'm too good a shot to get killed. Didn't I teach you, little brother? And look at that big old rabbit you got for supper." He tried to push Josh, who twisted away and plodded through the snow toward the farmhouse.

Even though Josh was cross with Jere for saying he was going off to war, he knew he would miss his brother. Jere had taught him almost everything he knew how to do. He had showed him how to shoot, teaching him to pour the powder down the musket barrel and tamp the ball down tightly, then place the cap to detonate the powder.

He had helped Josh shinny up the oak tree when Josh was just seven. Jere had made him climb out on the branch which grew over the pond, showing him how to stand on the knotted end of the big rope and wrap his arms and legs around tight and hold on. Then he had pushed Josh off the branch so that he swung way out over the pond. Josh had never been so scared in his life, but, after that first time, he had jumped off by himself without being pushed. How would he ever learn to be a man if Jere went away?

When Josh showed Mattie the rabbit, she snatched it away from him and danced around the room, singing a little song about rabbit stew.

Seated by the fire, The Man frowned. Taking a long draw from his whiskey jug, he set it down on the floor by his foot, grumbling, "Settle down, girl, and get that thing cleaned."

Mattie made a final pirouette, then froze in horror as her foot struck the jug, knocking it over and spilling amber liquid out across the bare wood floor.

"Now see what your foolishness has done," The Man fumed, rising. He slapped at Mattie, but the blow only glanced off her cheek. His great hand slammed into the china doll on the mantel, sending it smashing to the hearth.

Jere threw himself across the room onto The Man. Turning his wrath on Jere, The Man began to slap and pummel him, but Jere slipped beyond his reach.

What can I do, Josh cried inside, terrified, furious. He'll kill Jere if he catches him. Stepping toward The Man, he struggled to keep his voice from trembling. "Do you want me to get you another jug?"

The Man turned his reddened eyes on Josh and dropped his clenched fist. "Never mind. I'll get it myself." He stumbled from the house and went around in back to the barn.

Josh got a pan full of snow from outside. Wrapping some in a cloth, he held it to Mattie's cheek where a pinkish bruise was forming. She squirmed uncomfortably. "I know it hurts," he told her in a soothing voice, "but Mother used to do it and I know it will help."

In a little while, Mattie said she was all right and began to prepare supper. Josh blotted up the spilled whiskey while Jere picked up the pieces of the China doll and laid them on the mantel shelf.

When The Man returned, he lurched into the bed alcove and sat down heavily on the end of the bed to pull off his boots. "I'm going down river tomorrow," he slurred, not looking up. "Be gone about a week." Then he slumped down on the bed and began to snore.

After he was asleep, the children ate supper and made their plans, talking in quiet whispers at the table.

The Man left late the next afternoon. When they could no longer see him through the poplar branches, Josh and Jere dug the knapsack out of the barn floor. Mattie made a sling of her mother's shawl and wrapped her few personal belongings inside, tucking her rag doll in last so that just its black button eyes peeked out.

Putting his father's watch into his pocket, Jere handed the knapsack to Josh. They counted the gold coins again and put them back. Josh put in all the socks and underwear he and Jere shared, along with his heavy sweater, a clean shirt and his best homespun pants, with the suspenders still attached. The baptismal dress and the pictures went in last, with the big family Bible on top.

They went to bed early and tried to sleep, but all three tossed and turned all night, crawling out of bed before daylight crept across the sky. By lantern light, Mattie packed up some biscuits and dried apples and got jerky from the smokehouse while Josh and Jere went to the barn. Josh opened the side of the corncrib so the chickens could feast until The Man came home. Then he put a rope around the cow's neck and led her outside. They would have to leave her at the Hobb's farm so she could be milked. He went into the house to help Mattie, and in a few minutes Jere returned from the barn.

When the children were ready, they shut the heavy door of the cabin and climbed the hill to their mother's grave, standing close together while Josh said a small prayer. Then, Jere shouldered his musket and they left the farm, walking north on the river road. They tethered the cow to a tree at the lane that led up to the Hobb's farm. They didn't stop because they did not want to explain where they were going.

They walked all morning, stopping at noon to eat, then walked again until dusk turned to darkness. A farmer's wife gave them a hot meal and warm blankets and let them sleep in the barn for the night.

Without undressing, they wrapped in the blankets, snuggling close together in the straw to keep warm.

Suddenly, Mattie sat up. "You know what we forgot to do?" she blurted out.

"Lie down, Mattie. You're pulling the blankets off," Jere grumbled sleepily. A tugging match followed with Josh on one side and Jere on the other. In the middle, Mattie kept jabbing her brothers, saying, "We forgot . . . We forgot . . ."

"All right, what did we forget?" Jere asked finally.

"We forgot to smash The Man's jugs," Mattie moaned. "We were going to do that and we forgot."

"No, we didn't, Mattie," Jere chuckled. "That's why I stayed so long in the barn. I told you I would do it someday, and I did. Now hush and go to sleep."

The next morning they crossed the bridge over the boat canal and followed the wagons into Rochester. Four years ago they had come to the city with their mother to see Colonel Ellsworth and his marching cadets. Jere remembered how to get to Aunt Carrie's house. They finally found it on a narrow side street off East Avenue.

Their aunt and uncle's house was a large, two-story brick building with white pillars on either side of the front door. Hurrying up the stone walkway to the stoop, they rapped on the door with the heavy brass knocker and waited anxiously. Aunt Carrie opened the door, squealing with joy when she saw them and trying to hug them all at once.

"Mercy's sake!" she cried. "Let me look at you. Why—"

She drew in her breath sharply when she saw Mattie's cheek. A purplish bruise had formed where The Man had hit her. "What happened to you, darling?" she wailed.

Looking at Josh and Jere, she bleated, "You didn't . . . Oh, no, of course not. You wouldn't . . . What happened?"

She looked from one to the other. Jere explained about the miserable way The Man had behaved, and that was why they had brought Mattie to Rochester. He didn't say anything about his own plans, having explained to Josh that they should wait until Uncle was there.

At dinner they stuffed themselves with fried chicken, beans, and whipped potatoes, which the children scooped out in the middle and filled with rich brown gravy. There was pudding and a freshly baked cake for dessert. After dinner, when they were settled in the parlor, Josh had trouble keeping his eyes open, and Mattie fell asleep on the sofa with her head on Aunt Carrie's shoulder.

Jere explained to Uncle about The Man and why they had come to Rochester. He embellished the story, making The Man's behavior more lurid than it really had been. He kept saying, "Isn't that right, Josh? Isn't that what happened?" Josh nodded but said nothing. He thought The Man's behavior was bad enough without Jere's adding anything.

Finally, Jere cleared his throat and announced that he planned to enlist in the army the next day.

"What?" his aunt cried. "You'll do no such thing!"

"Now, Carrie, let him finish," Uncle said.

"You mustn't even think of going off to war." Aunt Carrie's anguished voice woke Mattie, who muttered and then went back to sleep.

Jere tried to explain, but Aunt Carrie kept interrupting. "Tell him he can't do that. Tell him he's too young," she spoke sharply to Uncle.

"I think your aunt is right, Jeremiah. I think you're about a year too young."

"But you said, yourself, that I'm big for my age. You said that last year, and I've grown since then. I bet the army will take me if they really need recruits."

"W . . e . . l . . l, they really do. Not many soldiers want to reenlist. And I must admit that I have heard of cases where boys as young as you have been taken in, but . . ."

"I'm going to enlist. I've made up my mind."

"You sound determined." Uncle looked nervously at Aunt Carrie.

Josh wanted to shout, "Can't you see he's serious? He's going to enlist tomorrow. But what about me? I promised Mother I would take care of him, and Mattie, too. How can I do that if he goes off to war and Mattie stays here?"

Jere opened the knapsack and took out the gold coins and the deed, showing them to his uncle and explaining about the fire and about hiding the knapsack so The Man wouldn't find their gold.

"We'll put this in the bank here where it will be safe and I'll talk to your stepfather. Maybe I can convince him to let you all stay here. I can threaten to have him thrown in jail for hurting Mattie."

"It won't work. He'll come after Josh and me and take us back, and that means Mattie will go, too. But, Aunt Carrie," Jere appealed to his aunt, "The Man didn't treat her right even before he hit her. Josh and I have decided that we can't let her go back there."

Josh nodded slowly. You never asked me, he thought, tears stinging his eyes. He turned his head. No! he would not cry. He had to be a man now if Jere were going to go away.

"I'll send you my pay every month for Josh and Mattie's keep," Jere continued, as if the matter were settled.

41

"No. No. If I can get your stepfather to let Joshua stay, he can work for me at the shop and Mattie, well, we are just delighted to have her here with us. You boys were right to bring her."

"I'll go tomorrow, sir. I want to get to the war before it's over," Jere continued.

"Well, I don't know how soon the war will be over, but I have to say I'm proud of you, Jeremiah," his uncle said. "Our army needs young men like you."

"Yes, sir," Jere smiled.

Josh thought angrily, Tell him, Jere. Tell him that you just want to get away, that you want to hear cannons booming up and down the valley.

Josh lay awake long after everyone else had gone to sleep that night. It would be nice to stay and live in this big, safe house and sleep every night between sweet-smelling sheets. This is where his mother had lived before she married his father. Did she sleep in these same soft sheets? I wish she were here now so that I could ask her what to do. I promised her I would do the right thing, but what is it? What should I do?

The next morning, Aunt Carrie cried all over again and pleaded with Jere and clung to him. Kissing her cheek, he put her aside and shook hands with Uncle, who gave him directions to the recruiting depot. Jere hugged Mattie and put his arm affectionately around his brother's shoulders. "I'm counting on you to take care of things now, Josh."

Then he left, striding down the cobblestone street to the corner and turning toward the center of town.

Mattie and Josh stood for a long time in front of the house after Aunt Carrie and Uncle went back inside.

Finally, Josh drew a deep breath and said, "Mattie, do you trust me?"

"Of course I do, Josh. You are my . . . You are the best . . . You're my best friend, and I love you," she finished in a rush of words.

"I love you, too, Mattie, and Aunt Carrie and Uncle love you. They will take good care of you if I . . ." He stopped, unable to tell her.

"What do you mean?" Mattie interrupted. "Oh! Josh, you're not going, too. You can't." Stricken, she stared at Josh.

"You know I am, don't you? You know that I have to go with Jere and take care of him."

"Oh, Josh. I can't bear it if you go," Mattie wailed.

"But you see why I have to go, don't you? I promised Mother I'd take care of both of you, but you don't need me as much as he does. You have people here who will take better care of you than I could. Jere wouldn't have anybody if I stayed."

"Oh, Josh." Tears filled Mattie's eyes.

"I promised Mother. She knew he was hot-headed. He needs me to keep him out of trouble."

Mattie slowly nodded. "I know."

A flood of relief swept over Josh. She did understand. She didn't like it; neither did he, but she understood. He was grateful for that.

"I don't think Aunt Carrie will let you go," she told him.

"Help me explain it to her," he pleaded.

Mattie had been right. Aunt Carrie said she was certainly not going to let both nephews walk out of her house and join the army. She and Uncle argued with Josh for almost an hour.

"You're only thirteen. That's too young."

"What would you do? You're not as tall as a musket."

"What if you and Jeremiah were both killed? That would leave your sister with no brothers at all."

But when Josh explained about the promise to his mother, Mattie took his side. Uncle finally said, "It's your decision, Joshua. If they will take you, I won't stop you from going. You have to do what you think is right."

"But you come right back if they won't take you," Aunt Carrie fussed.

Josh said he would and then added, "I don't think The Man will come if Jere and I aren't here. But if he does come, you won't let him take Mattie, will you?"

"Of course not!" Aunt Carrie and Uncle said together.

"Promise you'll write to me and tell me how you and Jere are getting along," Mattie said in a voice quivering with tears. Aunt Carrie rushed off to get him some paper and a pen and ink.

Josh went upstairs and got the knapsack. He put on his clean shirt and homespun pants, fastening the suspenders to hold them up. He put his father's knife in his pocket. Then he bundled up his farm clothes and carried them downstairs for Aunt Carrie to give away. He handed Mattie the Bible and the pictures, and he put the writing supplies into the knapsack on top of his underwear and socks.

"Who's going to darn your socks?" Mattie asked in a forlorn voice.

"I don't know. I expect I'll learn how." He wasn't really sure.

He hugged her quickly, hurrying out the door and down the street in the direction Jere had gone.

When Josh finally caught up with him, Jere was standing outside the army recruiter's office reading the signs posted on the building and in the windows. There were several men hanging around, talking and gesturing. A large soldier with a sunburned face and a sleeve full of yellow stripes was talking loudly to a group of fresh-faced young men and worried-looking store clerks. Nearby, an officer talked with a cluster of pretty young ladies. His gray horse nuzzled his arm and snorted, as if it were impatient to be off.

"Look! That sign says they pay a three-hundred dollar bonus!" Jere whistled. Then, realizing that it was Josh who stood next to him, he bellowed, "What are you doing here?"

Josh explained. At first, Jere was cross and told him to go home, but after a while he admitted he would be glad to have his little brother come with him, if they'd take him. They entered the recruiting office arm in arm. A sergeant with a big stomach greeted them pleasantly until he learned why they had come. Then he shook his head and said, no, he could not take both of them.

"You're all right," he nodded to Jere. "You're big enough to be sixteen, maybe seventeen." Then, winking at Josh, he chuckled, "But you, son, small as you are and with no fuzz on your face, I have a hard time believing you're old enough to be a soldier. You come back and see me in a year or two." His belly jiggled as he guffawed.

Jere put his arm around his brother's shoulders and announced, "It's both of us, or none at all."

"Well, now, I need one or two more men right now, today." The recruiter scratched his beard and thought for a moment, peering closely at Josh as though he might have aged while they were talking. Finally, his face brightened.

"Say, boy, can you play a drum? Can you tap a steady beat on a drum?"

"Uh, well . . . ," Josh mumbled. Jere's elbow dug into his ribs. "Well, yes, sir, as a matter of fact I can." Drumming his fingers on the table, he smiled hopefully.

The recruiter bobbed his head up and down encouragingly. "That's fine, that's fine. This company needs a drummer boy. You'll do. You'll both do."

★★ *Six* ★★

RECRUITS

A T noon on that same day, March 12, 1863, Joshua Parish, thirteen, and Jeremiah Parish, not quite sixteen, were sworn into a company of New York Volunteers.

The recruiter gave them each a blanket and a mess kit and told them to join the others in front of the recruiting office.

Captain Archibald Hale commanded the company. His young lady friends had left, and the captain was pacing back and forth, leading his horse.

Sergeant Willard was the company sergeant, the one with all the stripes on his sleeve. He was a veteran of many years in the army in Mexico and California. He had served under Captain Hale most of this time. He did not like new recruits, but he did his duty and got them ready to fight.

Sergeant Willard told Jere to go stand with the others. Then he took Josh over to a tall, skinny, young soldier who stood by himself. The soldier held a flag on a long pole in one hand. In the other, he held a large wooden drum with metal decorations.

"Private Eddie Boyd will show you what to do," the sergeant muttered and left Josh with the young soldier.

"I'm Joshua Parish," Josh introduced himself.

"Most people call me Eddie Boy because of my name," the young soldier explained, handing the drum to Josh.

Eddie Boy helped Josh get into the drum harness. He pulled a pair of drumsticks from his pocket and handed them to Josh.

"Do you know how to beat the drum?" he asked with a grin.

"Not really," Josh answered, grinning back.

"Most don't, to begin with. You'll learn quick enough. Just line up behind me when we start and give the drum some mighty whacks."

45

Josh tapped the drum a few times.

"You'll have to whack louder than that," Eddie Boy laughed. "They have to hear you all the way to Virginny."

I'll try, Josh thought and practiced whacking. He thought he should hit the drum slowly and evenly so the new recruits wouldn't have trouble marching. A steady beat, the recruiter had said.

Captain Hale mounted his horse and started slowly down the street. Eddie Boy followed, the flag fluttering in a slight breeze. Behind him, Josh struggled to get the drum to lie properly against his body. Then he fumbled with the drumsticks, dropping one and banging the drum on the cobblestones when he bent to pick it up.

Behind him, he heard Jere laugh. Then Sergeant Willard bellowed at the recruits, "Which is your left foot? Start with that. How many of you know which your left foot is?"

The recruits grumbled. Josh thought he heard Jere say something, but he wasn't sure. He was concentrating so hard on hitting the drum with the drumsticks and not dropping them that he forgot about Jere.

"Get together! Put your feet down smartly! Listen to me!" the sergeant bellowed.

The band of recruits shuffled out of town. Josh beat the drum as loudly as he could, but the sergeant kept yelling at him, "Louder!"

They marched south and east, away from Rochester and the Genesee River, away from the farm and everything Josh knew. The flat land swelled into small hills, and the marchers huffed and puffed, stopping often to rest.

Glaring at the panting recruits, the sergeant snorted, "You have to toughen up, behave like fighting men."

"It's easier for us," Jere said to Josh when they were resting. "We're used to walking behind the plow. Just look at that city boy." He pointed to a red-faced young man sitting nearby sketching with a pencil on a small pad of paper.

At noon, they ate their first taste of army rations—hardtack and beans cooked with a piece of hard jerky in a canteen split lengthwise to make a skillet. One of the veterans, a man named Hastings who had reenlisted for a second stretch, demonstrated the process.

As the mixture cooked, Josh sniffed hungrily. "Sure smells good."

Hastings served himself a generous portion and nodded to Josh to help himself. He shared the remains with Jere and the recruit with the sketch pad.

"Name's Wycoff." The recruit held out his hand.

"Jeremiah Parish," Jere said, shaking hands, "and this is my little brother, Josh. He came along to take care of me." He laughed and Josh blushed.

"I guess that's as good a reason as any of us has." Wycoff smiled at Josh.

"What were you drawing?" Josh asked shyly.

Wycoff tossed him a folded paper. "Here, send it home to your mother."

Josh studied the picture. With hundreds of little pencil lines, Wycoff had captured Josh's face on paper. He showed the picture to Jere. "That's you, little brother," Jere whooped. "The spittin' image."

"Thank you. I'll send it to my sister. Are you an artist?"

"Not really, but I work for the newspaper. The editor said I could send him sketches of the war sometimes. Said he might publish them."

"Up you go, boys," Sergeant Willard growled, moving among the groaning recruits. "Get along up there in front, Joshua Parish, and beat us a lively cadence for marching."

The captain cried, "Forward," and rode off toward the hills that loomed ahead. Eddie Boy followed, and Josh came along, pounding his drum mightily.

"Faster," Sergeant Willard ordered, coming up beside Josh. "Beat that drum faster. If you beat it slowly like that we won't be to Virginia before the war's over." Josh beat faster.

After a while, the sergeant came back and told him he was wearing out the leather on the drum. "Let 'em shuffle along at their own pace for a bit." Josh was glad to give his aching arms a rest.

They camped that night by a stream, falling asleep as soon as they had eaten. They marched all the next day and, at sunset, reached the southern tip of Seneca Lake. With blistered feet and aching muscles, the new recruits could barely swallow their rations before wrapping themselves in their blankets and sleeping.

The next day, as the sun warmed away the early morning mist, a band of twenty more recruits from the Seneca Lake region joined them. They were a noisy bunch, arguing and fighting among themselves, ready to take on anyone who looked crosswise at them.

"Make good soldiers," Josh heard the sergeant tell the captain. "Plenty of fight in 'em." Josh wondered how he could tell. The boys just looked mean to him.

The troop marched south along a little river that emptied into a broader river. Once, as they lay down to rest in tall grass, a flock of

47

Canada geese rose noisily from a nearby field. They circled slowly and flew north. Josh thought of Mattie's goose and was very lonesome the rest of the day.

At Elmira, they boarded a train loaded with recruits. Bouncing and jostling on wooden benches, they rode down through Pennsylvania to Washington, passing through the capital at night. The train crossed the Potomac River on the Long Bridge and stopped in Alexandria before daylight. Hundreds of new recruits poured out of the cars and formed their companies in the railroad yard.

The sun was up by the time Captain Hale's troop reached the sturdy wooden gates at Fort Ellsworth.

"Named for a great patriot," Captain Hale told Josh and Eddie Boy.

"I saw him four years ago in Rochester, sir, marching with his cadets on the Fourth of July," Josh said.

"And what did you think of him and his cadets, Joshua?" the captain asked.

"They looked . . . They marched . . ." What was it his mother had said when she saw their red pantaloons flashing, their bright gold buttons catching the July sun? "They marched very bravely," Josh told the captain.

"And is that the reason you enlisted? Because you wanted to march bravely like the Zouave cadets?" the captain asked, smiling tolerantly at Josh.

Josh didn't think he should tell the captain he had enlisted to take care of Jere, so he just said, "Yes, sir."

Sergeant Willard marched them under the sign, and they hurried through the busy fort. Armed soldiers patrolled in trenches, and mounds of earth protected the inner part of the fort, where the cannon were.

"Fort Ellsworth is part of the defensive circle of forts that protect our capital," the sergeant explained importantly, pointing across the river to the sprawling, white-marble city of Washington.

"I never thought . . . I didn't know . . . That sure is a big city!" Eddie Boy stammered.

Past the fort, they came to a camp of tents and buildings that stretched east over the rolling hills. Groups of soldiers hurried in every direction. Others lolled by campfires or crawled in and out of small tents that were set up on one side of an enormous, open field. On the other side were painted wooden buildings with signs reading

"Hospital" and "Headquarters" and "Quartermaster." They passed a building labeled "Stockade," and Sergeant Willard said he didn't want any of them to wind up in there.

He marched them out onto the open field and herded them into a neat square. "This is the parade ground," he growled, "so stand up straight and try to look like soldiers."

Josh could hear Jere, who was just behind him, whisper loudly to the recruit next to him, "Those Seneca Lake boys don't even have shoes. What kind of soldiers are they going to be?" The recruit, a friendly boy named MacNaughton, laughed.

Sergeant Willard hurried back to stand next to Jere, and the laughter stopped. Josh tried to stand as straight as he could and look soldierly.

In the center of the parade ground, another sergeant thundered, "You recruits are here to learn how to be soldiers, and it's my job to see that you do. You have just one month before you join the Army of the Potomac along the Rappahannock River, so you'd better learn fast. You'll have to follow commands and recognize bugle calls and load and fire your musket in thirty seconds. Your life may depend on these things."

Josh cringed when Jere whispered, "I already know all that."

The sergeant continued, "You flag bearers and musicians, you check in with the drum major over there. He'll show you what your duties are."

"Do we get to learn how to shoot, too?" Eddie Boy called out.

Sergeant Willard sighed and rolled his eyes. "The first thing *you* will learn is to speak only when you're spoken to." Then, softening a little when he saw how crestfallen Eddie Boy was, he added, "Maybe I'll teach you younguns how to load and fire when you finish your other duties. Might come in handy sometime."

Finally, the recruits were dismissed to find their tents and get a piping-hot meal at the mess area.

That night, Josh sat by the campfire and wrote to Mattie.

Fort Ellsworth, Virginia
March 20, 1863

My Dear Sister Mattie,
    We have finally arrived at Fort Ellsworth, where we will learn to be soldiers. At least, Jere will be a soldier. I am a drummer boy, because that was the

only way they would take me. It's not so bad. The sergeant is nicer to me and the color bearer, who carries the flag, than he is to the others. The color bearer's name is Eddie Boy, which is a good name because he talks like a boy although he is older than Jere.

Jere and I are in the same tent although at first we were assigned to different ones. Then Jere and his friend Mac got into a fight with two recruits from Seneca Lake who were in with them. Sergeant Willard decided Eddie Boy and I should share the tent with Jere and Mac and be a good influence on them. I am glad I came with Jere. He needs me, though he teases me about being his little mother instead of his little brother.

We ate a big meal first thing when we got here, having pork fried with onions and real biscuits, though they weren't as good as yours. Since we started on the march from Rochester, I have been getting so that I can eat anything. At first, hardtack biscuits almost choked me, but now I have learned how to eat them, and they even taste good to me. They are made of just flour and water, baked as hard as a rock.

One of my duties is to help the cooks. I peel potatoes and clean up. I did not join the army to be a cook, but I guess we all must do what is needed.

Captain Hale says tomorrow we will start our training. We have a lot to learn. I have already learned one bugle call, which is "Roast Beef" and is the call to dinner.

I am sending you a drawing that a friend made of me when we were marching here. His name is Wycoff and he works for *The Democrat*. If you see his pictures in the paper, look closely for your devoted brother,

Josh

Late that night, Jere and Mac crept into the tent after the bugle sounded "Lights Out." They brought the smell of whiskey with them

50

and shushed each other, giggling. "Blast!" Jere swore, groping for his blanket.

"You smell like The Man!" Josh hissed, but Jere did not answer.

The next morning, Jere and Mac sat with their heads in their hands and would not eat the eggs and greasy slabs of bacon and pancakes.

Drills began after breakfast. Jere was the only one with a musket, which he had brought with him from the farm. The other recruits used sticks and wooden brooms, whatever they could find, to drill with.

After a week, they got new muskets. Sergeant Willard watched them closely as they bit off the powder cap and rammed a minié ball down the barrel, aimed and fired. Jere earned the reputation as the best marksman. Since he had a new musket, he let Josh have his old one.

Josh drilled for hours with the other drummer boys and carried messages and worked in the mess tents. When he finished these duties, his friends taught him to play "base-ball" and he explored the fort with Eddie Boy. Sometimes they went to the firing range to practice with the older recruits.

After two weeks in camp, Captain Hale took his company on maneuvers out into the green Virginia countryside. He told them they had to listen for orders while they were running back and forth, this way and that. It would be like that in battle, he said. All morning they pretended to skirmish, falling on their bellies and firing into the empty woods, always listening for the captain's voice. Finally they stopped to rest in a field off the Falls Church Road. Gray squirrels played tag in the tall maple trees.

Jere and Mac lay side by side on the soft, moist ground while Josh ate his rations. Wycoff sat nearby sketching a graceful old house that stood at the end of a tree-lined drive. The house was dark inside, behind lace curtains.

"It's probably been deserted by secessionists," Wycoff said.

Eddie Boy asked, "What's a secessionist?"

"How do you know it's deserted?" Josh wanted to know.

"Got to be secessionists," Wycoff mused. "Why else would anyone leave such a beautiful place?"

"If they were secessionists, they're probably clear to Richmond with all their Confederate cousins by now," Hastings suggested.

"What's a secessionist?" Eddie Boy asked again

"Sure would be a lot of chores to do in a place that big," Josh decided.

"That's what they had slaves for," Wycoff explained. "To do the chores and work in the fields. See those little houses out back? That's where the slaves lived."

"Might even be some still hiding there," Hastings put in.

"What's a secessionist?" Eddie Boy demanded loudly, but no one answered.

Josh studied the little log cabins. They had no windows and only a small opening for a door.

What would it be like to live in there, he wondered. What would it be like to be a slave? Are there really slaves hiding in the cabins now, watching us eat? I wonder if they're hungry.

Are there children in there, too? What would children slaves do? They'd have to turn the hay in the barn stalls and walk behind the plow and hoe the weeds, just as we did. But they couldn't walk away, as we did. It would be like living with The Man . . . except that The Man didn't own us.

Back at camp that night, there was a letter waiting for him from Mattie. He found a quiet place and sat down to read it.

Rochester, New York
March 25, 1863

Dear Brother Josh,

Aunt Carrie is helping me write this letter because it is the first I have ever written. I have copied it three times already so that the words will be spelt correctly and the handwriting good so that you will be able to read it.

Thank you for the picture Mr. Wycoff drew. Please tell him I think he is a very good artist.

Your names were on the front page of *The Democrat,* you and Jere, and there was a picture drawn by Mr. Wycoff and an article about our local soldiers who have enlisted this month.

It said you were at Fort Ellsworth and told about Colonel Ellsworth coming to Rochester with his Zouave cadets in the summer of 1859. Do you remember the picnic we had when we saw them and how Aunt Carrie didn't want me to go back to the railroad station with you and Jere and the cadets, but I did anyway because Uncle said I could?

My teacher told Aunt Carrie that I am progressing well in my studies at school. My studies. Doesn't that sound grand? As though I was a student at a college. I think I would like to go to a college someday.

I hope you and Jere are safe. I know you are taking good care of him. I wish you were coming home soon because I miss you.

Aunt Carrie sends hugs and kisses to you and Jere, and of course I do, too. I hope you will write again soon to your loving sister,

Mattie

★★ *Seven* ★★

THE ROAD TO WAR

AFTER four weeks of marching and drilling, loading and firing, Captain Hale's company was ready to go to war. Each recruit was issued a uniform: blue wool pants, a coarse cotton shirt, and a loose-fitting jacket. There were boots that didn't fit and a cap with a small visor. Josh let Jere have some of the underwear and socks he had brought because the quartermaster had none in their size.

Jere said they were too small, but he took them anyway. "They're hand-me-hand-me downs," Josh grinned slyly.

Every soldier was given one piece of a two-man tent. He also carried his rifle, knapsack, food, and ammunition.

When they had buttoned their wool jackets, Jere saw that Josh's uniform was fancier than his plain one. It had light blue braid crisscrossing the chest, and there were twenty bright gold buttons down the front in three rows.

"Aren't you the handsome one!" Jere snorted. His own jacket hung on him like a gunnysack and had just five buttons.

"Handsome is as handsome does," Josh smirked.

Jere stomped away in his big, new boots to look for Mac. They returned with a small, cracked mirror and took turns admiring themselves.

"They say we're off tomorrow," Mac said eagerly.

"At last!" Jere exclaimed, swaggering around.

"I don't know why you're so excited," Josh said.

"Don't be so serious, little mother. This is going to be an adventure for all of us. You'll see."

They left Fort Ellsworth the next morning, winding through Alexandria and down along the Potomac. Captain Hale pointed to a two-story brick hotel, The Marshall House. "That's where your hero,

Colonel Ellsworth, was shot by secessionists, Josh. It's a famous place now."

"What's a secessionist?" Eddie Boy asked just as they passed a large building with the words PRICE BIRCH & CO., DEALER IN SLAVES lettered in white above the door. "Will you look at that!" Eddie Boy exclaimed. "You'd never see the likes of that back in Rochester."

"No," Josh answered patiently. "They don't have slaves in Rochester."

Eddie Boy told everyone that Josh was his best friend. Josh had never had a friend before, except Jere and Mattie. He liked Eddie Boy, who was eighteen, although he realized that Eddie Boy was slow to understand things.

As they started south on the Telegraph Road, it began to drizzle, slowing them down, making the long morning march longer. When they stopped to rest and eat, Josh slumped down next to Jere under a broad tree and unwrapped his noon meal of hardtack and a bit of salt meat that Cook had given him before they left Alexandria. He held out the hardtack to catch some raindrops, then began to massage it in his mouth.

Biting off a piece of salt meat, he popped it into his mouth to mix with the hardtack and saliva.

"That's horse you're eating," Ruggles laughed from his place under a nearby tree. "Salt horse."

"Then you don't want any," Josh called back and passed the meat to Jere and the others.

Reaching down by the toe of his boot, Jere picked up a dead, bloated toad and tossed it into Ruggles' lap. "Here's some fresh meat for you," he crowed. Everyone guffawed except Ruggles, who made a rude gesture in Jere's direction.

"Did you see that creek . . . that creek we just passed back there?" Eddie Boy faltered. "Looked like the one where my gramma lives when it floods in the spring—all muddy and wild." He added, frowning, "I can't swim, you know."

"Too bad," Ruggles cackled. "We'll have to swim the Rappahannock when we get there." Eddie Boy's sunburned face immediately turned pale.

"And . . . it's . . . full . . . of . . . water moccasins." Ruggles spoke slowly, cruelly.

"Don't listen to him. He's just a bully," Josh said.

Mac spoke up. "I've got a cousin lives near Culpeper."

"That's over by the mountains," Wycoff said.

"He must be a Johnny Reb," Mac chuckled. "Wouldn't it be funny if we got to shooting at each other."

"It wouldn't be the first time. Back in camp I was talking to a soldier who fought against his own brother at Fredericksburg last winter. One was a Yankee, the other a Johnny Reb." Wycoff shook his head as though he could not understand it.

"Did they kill each other?" Eddie Boy asked, his blue eyes anxious.

"Of course they did! And their ghosts told Wycoff all about it," Ruggles hooted. Eddie Boy grinned good-naturedly.

"Wish we were headed back to Seneca Lake," Ruggles said to no one in particular.

"Why's that, barefoot boy?" Jere laughed. Unaccustomed to wearing shoes, Ruggles had taken off his boots and was wiggling his toes in the mud.

"The sooner I get away from you farm clods and back to my sweetheart, the better," Ruggles shot back.

"You mean there's some barefoot girl back home just panting to wiggle her toes in the mud with you?" Jere grinned and the others applauded.

After a while the banter stopped. Jere and Mac whispered softly, and Josh dozed against the tree. Suddenly, bugle notes interrupted his nap. "To the march!" the bugle blared. He jumped to his feet and shook himself awake. My responsibility! I have to get them started. Snatching up his drum and sticks, he raced to the road.

"Step lively now, boy," Captain Hale said. "We need you to tap out a lively pace if we're going to cover another ten miles in this mud today. You know that new battle hymn they're singing?"

"Yes, sir. We learned it in camp," Josh answered, stepping into line.

"Well, tap that out. That'll get them singing. Easier to march when you're singing. You, Sergeant Willard, get them started," the captain ordered.

Josh tapped smartly on his drum and Sergeant Willard began to sing in a resounding bass voice.

> *Mine eyes have seen the glory of the coming*
> *of the Lord,*

Others joined in quickly.

> *He is trampling out the vintage*
> *where the Grapes of Wrath are stored,*
> *He has loosed the fateful lightning*
> *of His terrible swift sword,*
> *His Truth is marching on.*
>
> *Glory, glory, Hallelujah,*
> *Glory, glory Hallelujah,*
> *Glory, glory Hallelujah*
> *His Truth is marching on.*

When they finished, they sang it over again. Over and over, the same words, the same steady beat.

Later, the rain turned to drizzle. They crossed Acquia Creek and came to a silent farmhouse. There seemed to be no one around. Looking back, Josh saw Jere hand his musket to Mac and climb over the rail fence alongside the road. Standing on tiptoe, Jere reached for some late-winter apples still caught in the branches of a tree.

A plump girl stepped out on the farmhouse porch and called to Jere, "What, Yankee boy, have you come to steal away my apples?" Tossing her fair hair, she planted her hands firmly on her round hips, her wide smile belying her cross words.

Flustered, Jere's face turned shades of red, but he managed to hang on to most of the apples. "Yes, Ma'am. As a matter of fact I've come to steal a kiss if you have one to—"

A screeching hag of a woman flew out of the house and seized the plump girl, sending her inside with a slap on her plump behind.

"Get off my land, you Yankee thief," she crowed, rushing down the steps and scooping up a handful of rotting apples from the ground. With deadly aim, she pelted the startled Jere, one apple catching him squarely on the cheek.

Jere wiped his face with his sleeve. "I'm going, I'm going. Look, old lady, I'm gone," he laughed. Vaulting the fence, he ran to catch up with Mac in line.

"She got you good," Mac taunted, handing Jere back his musket.

"Silly old crone," Jere laughed, "but did you see her daughter?"

"She'll look just like that old hag in a few years, withered and dry like those apples," Ruggles called from behind.

"But she doesn't now!" Jere countered. "She's round and sweet," he bit into one of the apples, "like these apples." Smacking his lips noisily, he handed an apple to Mac.

Rain and mud made the going slow, so the captain called an early halt. The drenched soldiers pitched their tents and settled down to dinner rations—hardtack soaked in hot coffee.

Jere and Mac had their heads together, laughing, nudging each other. Josh heard Jere say, "That girl back there deserves a Yankee kiss, don't you think?" Mac nodded.

Josh crawled closer to Jere and whispered, "You can't go back there. If the sergeant finds out you're gone, you could wind up in the stockade."

"There's no stockade out here, little mother. Now shush, or we'll have the whole camp coming with us." Slowly, Jere got up and sauntered away from the fire. A few minutes later, Mac followed, whistling.

Eddie Boy spoke timidly, "I heard the captain say General Hooker hisself is waiting for us up ahead."

"I heard tell the president and Mrs. Lincoln are there, too," Hastings answered, lighting his pipe.

"No!" Ruggles scoffed.

"I heard the captain say that, too," Eddie Boy agreed.

"Well, it must be true if *you* heard the captain say it," Ruggles snickered sarcastically.

Darkness crept through the trees and surrounded them. A night bird called a sad, clear song.

"Bad luck," a young recruit warned.

"What?" Eddie Boy moaned. "What's bad luck?"

"Whippoorwill," the recruit answered. "When you hear that bird at night, something bad's going to happen."

Eddie Boy looked around. Taking out his harmonica, he blew a few mournful notes, like the song of the whippoorwill. The music drifted into a tune the men knew, and they began to sing.

> *Many are the hearts that are weary tonight,*
> *Tenting on the old camp ground . . . .*

Josh took out his pen and paper. Using his drum as a table, he began to write.

On the road to
Fredericksburg
April 20, 1863

Dear Sister,

I received a letter from you before we left Fort
Ellsworth but could not write sooner because we
were very busy preparing to leave. I am pleased that
you are doing well in school. If you are going to go
to a college someday, you will surely have to study
hard now.

When we left camp yesterday we passed
through Alexandria and could see the capital of
Washington across the river. The captain showed us
Marshall House, where Colonel Ellsworth was shot.
You asked whether I remember the time we saw
him, and you followed Jere and me to the railroad
station. You were quite a tomboy then. You probably are not anymore, now that you live in the city.

We went down another street, and there was a
building three stories high built of brick with the
sign Price Birch & Co., Dealer in Slaves. I have
tried to imagine what the life of a slave would be
like and how it would feel to actually be owned by
someone. Some of the men say we are fighting this
war because of slavery, and I guess that is a good
reason to fight, though I never thought much about
it before.

I dare not say this to the others, even Jere, because I think they would laugh at me. You are probably the only person who would not think I am
foolish because of all the questions in my mind. I'm
glad I can write to you. Otherwise I would have to
keep it all inside me.

I'll ask Jere to write something when he comes
back. He and Mac have gone off together on some
adventure.

Jere and Mac suddenly appeared beside Josh at the fire and thrust
something hard and lumpy at him. "Hide this," Jere hissed.

Sergeant Willard scowled at them from the other side of the fire. "Been out foraging, boys?"

"We've just been over there for a friendly game of poker," Mac lied, pointing to a neighboring tent where some men sat cross-legged on the ground playing cards.

Josh looked at the lumpy thing in his lap. It was an enormous sweet potato. Jamming it quickly into the embers of the dying fire with a stick, he smiled weakly at the sergeant who turned to look at him.

"Well, mind you stay in camp, boys," the sergeant spoke sternly. "The captain doesn't allow foraging. Besides, you need your rest. Reveille is at five tomorrow. We should reach Falmouth Camp by midday." The sergeant stood up, stretched, and moved away.

Later that night in their tent, Jere explained that the pickets had challenged them before they reached Acquia Creek, so they never got to the apple lady's place. Their only adventure was to steal a sweet potato from a nearby farm.

Josh finished his letter to Mattie and handed Jere a piece of paper and the pencil.

"Write something," he ordered. Propping the writing paper on his knee, Jere wrote,

> We have just finished a feast of hot sweet potato, enough for all of us, and I am the one who provided it.
>
> Your little friends at school must think you are very lucky to have two handsome brothers off at the War.
>
> I will write a better letter soon as I get an opportunity. Josh hasn't given me much paper, and we are supposed to go to sleep because the bugler has played taps, and we must be on the road early.
>
> From your brave brother,
>
> Jeremiah Parish

The next day they reached Falmouth Camp, which was just across the Rappahannock River from the Confederate camp at Fredericksburg. It was bigger than Fort Ellsworth, with a sea of tents sprawling across hills and grassy fields. There were wooden buildings, too, and a beautiful old house that served as a hospital. Flags and

61

brightly colored pennants snapped in the wind around a broad parade ground where the grass was all trampled down.

Across the wide river, Confederate soldiers moved around their camp.

"They don't look like the enemy, do they?" Josh asked Jere as they unrolled their tent. "They look just like me . . . and you . . . and the sergeant."

"That's treason, little brother," Jere warned, jokingly. "That's the enemy over there, and don't you forget it."

"They don't look much like the enemy," Josh argued. "See there, that big one with the red hair looks just like the sergeant." Jere peered across the river and laughed."And the boy over there, the one with the drum. That's me," Josh continued.

"I see him. The one with all the gold buttons. But he's a Reb—"

"Look, there's one wiping his face with his sleeve, just like you do. He looks just like you." The brothers laughed.

"Darned if he don't. Hey, there, Johnny Reb!" Jere shouted across the river. The young Confederate soldier lifted his head in surprise, looked at Jere, and waved.

"Hey there, Billy Yank!" he shouted back.

Sergeant Willard hurried toward them, bellowing, "Stop that hollering and get your tent up, you two." The boy across the river laughed loud enough for them to hear.

"Yes, sir," Josh and Jere chorused.

When they looked across the river again, Johnny Reb was gone. Jere punched Josh's shoulder. "You're supposed to be looking out for me, and here you almost got me in trouble with Sarge," he chided.

When their tents were up and their gear stowed inside, Jere and Mac went off to look around camp for some excitement. Josh found a quiet place to read a letter that was waiting for him from Mattie.

> Rochester, New York
> April 10, 1863
>
> My Dear Brother, Josh
> The newspaper says that many of our local boys have moved to the Rappahannock River and will probably see battle there, so I wonder whether you and Jere are going there now. I shall send this letter and hope it finds you. I have not had any letter

from you in three weeks. Uncle says if you are on the move, the mails may be slow.

On Saturday last, I went with Aunt Carrie to the Ladies' Hospital Auxiliary, which meets in a big house on East Avenue, across from the park where we saw Colonel Ellsworth's cadets. We wrapped bandages—yards and yards of bandages, miles and miles of bandages—until my arms were sore. The ladies kept saying what a good helper I was and how I was doing this for my dear brothers who were away at war. They smiled and fussed over me and told me how pretty and brave I was. I am getting very spoilt.

Some of the ladies sat in a corner whispering about a book called *Uncle Tom's Cabin* written by Mrs. Stowe. It's a story about Negro slaves and how badly they are treated. Aunt Carrie said they should not be talking of such things around a child, which made me quite angry because I am not a child. I did not say another word to her until we came home. Then I asked her to buy a copy of the book so I could read it. She was horrified and refused, saying I should read *Cinderella's Glass Slipper,* which she had gotten for me. But Uncle said that any girl who had two brothers fighting in a war against slavery should know what an evil practice it is. He went straight downtown to buy a copy and helped me read the first few pages. It is very hard to read because the life of the slaves is so terrible. Aunt Carrie lets me read it now, but she has made me promise I will not tell anyone what I am reading.

So you must promise not to tell on your sister,

Mattie

When he finished reading, Josh put the letter in his knapsack and went to look around the bustling camp. His company had been assigned to a regiment of New York Volunteers, nearly a thousand soldiers, already there in camp. The regiment was part of General

Meade's Fifth Corps. Standing alone at one end of the parade ground, the general's tent was guarded by two armed sentries. They challenged anyone who came near.

Josh saw Sergeant Willard talking to Eddie Boy and joined them. "You see, every company and regiment, every division and corps has its own flag, and you better learn which ones are yours so you don't get lost. You'll have to know that in battle, too."

Eddie Boy nodded agreeably as the sergeant named the flags they should recognize, then told them to go off and look around. "And keep out of trouble," he warned.

They walked up and down the dusty paths between the tents, stopping to talk with soldiers gathered around fires, playing cards or gossiping. They passed the mess tents and, finally, came to a woods at the far end of camp.

"Look up yonder!" Eddie Boy gasped, pointing to the treetops.

Above their heads, a huge, gray balloon rose up over the trees and hovered in the cloudy sky. Long ropes secured it to the ground behind the trees. Small figures peered over the edge of a little basket that hung below the balloon.

Josh and Eddie Boy raced back toward the regiment, looking for Jere or Mac or someone they could tell about the wonderful sight they had seen.

"Look there!" Josh panted when he saw Captain Hale. "What's that, captain?" The captain smiled. "That's a spy balloon, Josh. We send them up when the weather's clear enough to scout the enemy. The Rebs have them, too."

"Who rides in the little basket? What happens if the balloon gets shot? How do they get back down if the ropes break?" The boys were full of questions.

"Slow down, lads," the captain said. "You will have to find out for yourselves. Look around over at the launch area. Maybe someone there can answer your questions."

But when Josh and Eddie Boy went back to the trees, a guard waved them away. "You can't go over there," he told them importantly.

"We just want to get a closer look at the balloon," Josh explained.

"We're not spies," Eddie Boy added. "We just want—"

"Get away, you two. Now!" The guard puffed himself up, making himself look bigger, and thrust his musket across his chest.

As they walked away, disappointed, they met Jere and Mac.

"Did you see that balloon?" Eddie Boy greeted them.

"See it! We got ourselves a ride in it," Jere laughed.

"Be serious, Jere. You can't get within a mile of that balloon." Josh laughed, too.

"*We* can. We talked the professor into giving us a little ride."

"Who's the professor?" Eddie Boy wanted to know.

"He flies the balloon," Mac told them. "He rides in the little basket under the balloon and draws pictures showing where the Reb troops are moving."

"We saw people in the basket . . ." Eddie Boy stopped. "Was that *you?* Were *you* in the basket?" Turning to Josh, he said excitedly, "That was *them* we saw."

Jere and Mac bragged about all they had seen, the Rappahannock River winding west to the Blue Ridge Mountains which disappeared up north near the Potomac River. They said they'd seen Confederate camps and the dust of troops moving.

I don't believe you, Josh thought. You're just making it up.

✯✯ *Eight* ✯✯

AMBUSH

THE bugler blasted 'Reveille' before daylight. Stumbling from their tents, Josh and Eddie Boy dressed and joined hundreds of soldiers in lines moving past tables set up in front of the mess tents. They got a heaping spoonful of lumpy oatmeal mush, a slab of pink bacon, pancakes, and hot, strong coffee in their tin mugs.

Jere and Mac came along late, after all the pancakes were gone, complaining loudly as they sat down. Josh slipped his last pancake onto Jere's plate, and Jere nodded thanks.

After breakfast, their regiment formed by companies. Around them, other regiments formed until the parade ground was filled with men and flags and the sound of sergeants calling out orders.

General Meade strode briskly from his tent and frowned at the assembled troops. His great hooked nose, his leathery skin, and his popping eyes gave him the look of a snapping turtle, which was what the men called him outside his hearing. The general spoke to his officers but did not address the men. After he returned to his tent, the officers spoke to their sergeants, and the sergeants turned to face their companies.

"We are departing within the hour," Sergeant Willard bellowed. "We will move up the Rappahannock behind the hills and reach Kelly's Ford sometime tomorrow."

As it grew light, the soldiers marched away from Falmouth Camp, leaving the river shrouded in mist. Josh started out with a steady cadence, then stopped and let the men move along at their own pace, in route step, slower, easier.

A blazing sun burned away the mist, leaving behind moisture so heavy in the air that it formed droplets that mixed with sweat on their faces and ran down their necks inside their shirt collars. Some men collapsed to rest in the long grass by the roadside, then had to hurry to catch up. Many shed their jackets or left blankets lying beside the road rather than carry them with their knapsacks and muskets and ammunition.

Storm clouds gathered suddenly, and they were drenched with rain.

From behind, a bugle sounded. They moved aside as a group of soldiers rode down on them in the rain, a general and his staff on glistening horses. The general's hair stuck out from under his wide-brimmed hat, and his fierce eyes looked straight at Josh as he rode past, his horse prancing and throwing up globs of mud.

In spite of the mud, in spite of their tired feet and aching shoulders, the soldiers cheered. They recognized General Hooker, the new commander of the Army of the Potomac. They cheered until he disappeared back into the rain farther down the road.

Slipping up behind Josh, Jere whispered excitedly, "Did you see him? Did you see 'Fighting Joe' Hooker?"

"I saw him," Josh grumbled. "His horse splattered mud all over me."

"That's an honor, little brother," Jere beamed. "He's going to lead us to victory, right now, right here along the Rappahannock."

As the men began to march again, they sang. First one bass voice, then more, then all.

> *The Union boys are marching on the left*
> *   and on the right,*
> *The bugle call is sounding, our shelters*
> *   we must strike.*
> *Joe Hooker is our leader, he takes his*
> *   whiskey strong,*
> *So our knapsacks we will sling and we'll go*
> *   marching along.*

They marched all day, rested at night, and started out again as the sun rose the next morning. The road wound back to the river, which was swollen now with muddy water from the rain.

At midday, they stopped to rest and eat hardtack, washed down with hot coffee.

"What I wouldn't give for one of those sweet apples we got back at Acquia Creek," Jere told Mac.

Ambush

"And the apple lady's sweet daughter," Mac prompted. They dissolved into laughter, rolling in the grass and kicking their heels in the air.

"You act like little boys," Josh scolded. Leaving them, he went down to the river to wash up, slipping on the muddy bank and catching branches to save himself from the wild water.

As he emerged from the trees, two Negroes scrambled up from where they crouched by the river. Josh stared. He had never seen Negroes up close before.

One was a huge man with glistening, black skin and tightly knotted hair. The other was a young boy, maybe eight or nine. Trembling, the boy's dark eyes locked on Josh's.

"What's your name?" Josh blurted out, but the boy did not answer.

"He don't talk," the man said, placing his hand gently on the boy's shoulder. "Not since they caught his mama and his sister, he ain't said a word."

Josh had heard talk of slaves who ran away from their owners and the terrible things that happened if they were caught. Maybe these were runaways.

"Are you going north?" he asked. The man nodded.

"How do you know which way to go?"

"We following the bright star at night. It shines right down into the drinking gourd and shows us the way north. We follows it, and we be safe."

A bugle called to Josh, but he did not move. Shuffling feet started down the road.

"I have to go now. I hope you find where you are going." Reaching into his pocket, he pulled out some taffy Cook had given him back at Fort Ellsworth and held it out to the boy, but fear lingered, and the boy shrank behind the man.

"Good luck," Josh said, handing the man the candy and scrambling up the bank.

"You're late," Jere chided when he returned to the road. "What kept you?"

When Josh explained, Mac drew in his breath sharply. "You touched him? What did his skin feel like?"

"I dunno, like yours, I guess. How should it feel?"

"Shiny. Smoother and shinier than mine," Mac answered.

"Probably feels like anybody else's skin, unless you're in it," Wycoff suggested.

69

The road narrowed. They marched in single file now, careful not to slip down the bank to the river. Brambles tore at their clothes, and mosquitoes tormented them. Stopping at sunset, they ate again, rested again, then moved on. When it was dark, Josh stopped to look for the stars the Negro man had told him about. He found the bright North Star and the Big Dipper, shaped like a drinking gourd. He thought of the man and the little boy and wondered whether they were looking at the stars, too. When a whippoorwill cried in a thicket near him, he shivered. Why am I afraid? For myself or for them? Pushing the fear back down inside, he caught up with the others.

They reached Kelly's Ford at ten o'clock that night and found that a pontoon bridge had been laid on small boats across the river. Even the strongest soldiers were relieved that they didn't have to flounder in the raging river.

Once across the Rappahannock, they camped for the night. All the next day, they pushed their way through thickets, reaching the Rapidan River at dusk. This river was smaller, and they had to wade across.

In the middle, Eddie Boy slipped on the rocks and would have been swept away in the current, but Jere grabbed him by the shirt and dragged him to the other side. Ruggles reached a hand down to pull them up. Eddie Boy handed him the flagpole, then scrambled up the bank by himself.

"No water moccasins?" Ruggles laughed, thumping the sputtering boys on the back.

Gnats filled their mouths and got in their eyes and ears, and thorns from wild blackberry bushes scratched their hands and faces. Mosquitoes bit them. They struggled on, grumbling and cursing.

Even Mac complained crossly, "Where's the adventure in this?"

"We're on the Rebs' side of the river now," Jere answered him cheerfully. "Now we'll get into the fight!"

"Or into our graves," Mac snorted.

"Or both," Wycoff suggested.

The next morning when they woke, their wet blankets were frozen to the ground. They sat by the fire all day, drinking coffee, trying to get warm.

"Why are we waiting?" Jere worried impatiently. "What's holding us back?" He jumped up, spilling Hastings's coffee.

"Watch what you're doing!" Hastings cried out angrily. "There'll be plenty of Rebs for you soon enough."

Toward evening, Jere and Mac went out on the picket line to help guard the camp for the night.

"Keep a sharp lookout," Sergeant Willard warned. "The Rebs are near, so stay quiet and alert."

"Yes, yes," Jere grumbled impatiently.

"Sleep well, lads. We'll watch out for you," Mac called as they left camp.

But Josh slept restlessly, waking often to think about Jere, then dozing again. Before dawn he heard a whippoorwill. Shivering, he burrowed deep into his damp blanket.

In the morning, mist clung to the branches of the trees. They ate hardtack and jerky and drank more coffee. Then, taking the last sheet of dry paper from his pouch, Josh laid it on the drumhead and began a letter to Mattie, writing small, crowding his words together.

> Somewhere south of the
> Rappahannock
> May 2, 1863

He stared at the paper, wondering how to describe what he was feeling. Nervous about Jere. Excited because the Rebs were close by. Waiting. Waiting for the war to start. For him. For all of them.

> Dear Sister Mattie,
> We have just finished a hard march from Fredericksburg to this place, which is south of Kelly's Ford on the Rappahannock River and south of the Rapidan, too. Sometimes we were in mud up to our knees. When the mud dried, we were so covered with dust our own friends could not recognize us.
> I want to tell you about something that happened to me yesterday. I went down to the edge of the river to wash up. There were two runaway slaves there, one a little boy who would not say a word to me. The other was a very big man. I don't think he was the boy's father. He said the boy had not talked since his mother and sister had been caught. And killed, I guess. It made me realize how I would feel if something like that happened to you and how awful the life of a slave must be.

I wonder who would kill that boy's mother and
his sister. Why does he have to be afraid? How can
one person own another? What would it feel like to
be owned? I used to think The Man owned us or at
least that our life was unbearable with him, but it
wasn't so terrible after all. This boy's life is worse,
and so was his sister's. Write and tell me if you
agree with me. I miss having you to talk to, and it
makes me proud when I get your letters at mail call.

This morning before dawn I heard a whippoorwill call. It is a very sad song and sends chills up
my spine since someone told me it is a bad omen.
I'm afraid something bad will happen to Jere while
he is out on guard duty.

Josh stopped writing and listened to Eddie Boy play his harmonica. Laying his letter aside, he rested.

Wycoff and Hastings came to him on their way out to replace Jere
and Mac.

"Keep my paper and pencil for me?" Wycoff asked Josh, handing
him a packet of paper folded around his pencil. "I won't be drawing
out there. Have to watch out for the enemy."

"Better keep my matches, too," Hastings said. "Put them in that
waterproof bag of yours in case it rains, will you? Sarge says no fires
out there."

Josh stuffed their things into his pouch, which he then pushed
down into his coat pocket between the hardtack and sweet taffy he
had there.

When Jere and Mac returned to camp, they were covered with
mosquito bites and bramble scratches. Without a word, Jere stretched
out by the fire and closed his eyes. Mac soaked his handkerchief in
cool water and covered the bites and scratches on his face.

"This is better," Jere sighed. "It surely was hard to stay awake out
there, even with mosquitoes biting me all night long."

"We heard Rebs when we first got there," Mac said. "I called to
'em and asked if they knew my cousin from over by Culpeper."

"But Sarge told you to be quiet," Josh protested.

"Why? They were talking to us," Jere laughed. "Anyway, pretty
soon they started laughing and taking pot shots at us so we hightailed
it out of there and found a more peaceful tree to sit under."

Josh was relieved that Jere was safe. He stretched his legs toward the fire and gently snapped his suspenders against his stomach, a relaxing sound. Across the fire, Jere and Mac laughed and whispered, then went back to cleaning their rifles.

Ruggles took a folded handkerchief out of his pocket, opened it and took out a single auburn curl of hair which lay hidden in the linen folds. He fingered the curl gently, then folded it in his handkerchief again and put it away.

Eddie Boy began to play his harmonica. Two or three men sang.

> *Many are the hearts that are weary tonight,*
> *Wishing for the war to cease.*
> *Many are the hearts looking for the right*
> *To see the dawn of peace.*
> *Tenting tonight, tenting tonight,*
> *Tenting on the old camp ground.*

A deer bounded into the clearing. Leaping high over Josh's outstretched legs, it dashed off into the woods on the other side of the fire. Startled, everyone looked around, then settled back down.

> *We've been tenting tonight*
>   *on the old camp ground,*
> *Thinking of the days gone by,*
> *Thinking of the loved ones—*

A single shot rang out. Then a sound between a yell and a scream came from a hundred throats, from the forest, from the very trees themselves. It trapped them, freezing them where they were.

Shots exploded everywhere, and hundreds of howling Rebels swarmed from the trees around them. Paralyzed, Josh watched in horror as Jere clutched his chest and slumped sideways to lean on Mac whose face had been shot away. Their bodies fell together into the fire.

Suddenly the men around him moved, scrambling for cover, leaving Josh alone by the fire. Some dragged their rifles with them, trying to load and shoot, but Rebel bullets found their mark and the men fell, one by one. The *thud, thud* of bullets as they hit, the shouts and screams of pain seemed to fade away. As though he were dreaming, Josh crawled slowly to Jere and pulled his body from the fire, which had gone out.

Like Jere, he thought. Like his life. Like his blue eyes, gone out now. Horror turned to fury.

Seizing a musket, he rose and swung it at the nearest Rebel face. He felt bone crush. Again and again he swung the musket. Gasping, smashing, he beat his way toward the trees. Then, throwing down the musket, he stumbled past a small dogwood tree whose flowering branches reached out to embrace him. Confused, blinded by tears, he crashed into a gigantic oak tree and spun around as the rough bark tore at his skin. He clawed his way through thick pines, away from the terrible cries of the dying, away from the *pop, pop* of muskets firing, and above all and everything, away from the Rebel yell.

Deep and deeper into the Wilderness he plunged until the trees blotted out the awful sounds of death. Dropping to the forest floor, he howled like a wild animal.

"I didn't help him!" he cried over and over.

"I didn't help him," filled the forest.

✩✩ *Nine* ✩✩

THE WILDERNESS

I didn't help him!" The words pulsed through Josh like his heartbeat. He couldn't see because his eyes were stuck shut from tears that had dried. He rubbed them and saw that the forest was growing lighter. It gets light in the east, he thought. Where Jere is. He slipped back into a fitful sleep.

He was in camp again, and Jere was laughing by the fire. Shots crashed around him and sounded *thud, thud* as the minié balls found their mark. He pressed his hands over his ears to keep out the sound, but the shots struck him, shattering him, and they would not stop. Finally, the sound of shooting faded, draining everything inside away until there was nothing left of him.

"What am I going to do?" he cried out loud. "Help me. *Help me!*" The forest echoed, "Help me!"

He slept again and dreamed of his mother's voice. "Behold, I send my messenger before thy face. . . . The voice of one crying in the wilderness. . . ."

When he woke it was night. The camp and Jere and the shooting were far away, like something that had happened to him a long time ago. Climbing to his feet, he stumbled forward, bumping into trees and falling to the ground again. He closed his eyes. Tight. Tighter. But the tears came anyway.

It was daylight when he opened his eyes again. How long have I been here, he wondered. Days? A week? His stomach groaned. I'm hungry. How can I be hungry?

Sitting up, he took everything out of his pockets, examining each object, then setting it on the ground in front of him. The waterproof pouch, with Wycoff's paper and pencil and Hastings' matches, some

75

hardtack biscuits and taffy, and a partly eaten chunk of jerky. Salt horse, Ruggles had called it. Was he dead, too?

He put a piece of taffy into his mouth and dug deeper, finding a length of candle and his knife and the new boot laces he had gotten a week ago. He had never put them in his boots.

Biting off a piece of hardtack, he chewed it with the lingering sweetness of the taffy. It's good I have the matches and the knife. Maybe I can catch something and cook it. What can I catch around here? If I make a trap, maybe I can catch a bird or a rabbit. If I had a hook, I could catch a big old catfish. If there's a stream around here someplace, there'll be catfish in it. What could I use to make a fishhook?

Unconsciously, he began to plan what he should do. Have they given me up for dead? What will happen to me if I don't go back? I'll be a deserter. What then?

I can't stay here. Where can I go? Can I find my way to Rochester? Will Uncle let me stay if I'm a deserter? Fear tightened around his chest. What will Mattie think? Will she blame me for not helping Jere? Oh, please, no. Don't let her blame me. I tried to take care of him, but I couldn't. I couldn't stop the shooting. I couldn't stop the bullet that killed him. I tried, but I just couldn't take care of him.

Then he remembered what his mother had said: "You will need to search your heart for what is right." Immediately, he felt the fear and uncertainty slipping away and knew he would not go back to the camp. He would go to Rochester, traveling at night so nobody would see him, and sleeping in the daytime. Like the Negro man and the silent boy, he would follow the North Star and the Big Dipper.

If I can find a farm around here, there might be a shirt and pants hanging on a clothesline. And some food, too. This is Confederate territory. Which would be worse, getting caught stealing by a Confederate farmer or being picked up by Union soldiers as a deserter? Would they hang a thirteen year old for desertion?

He ate the rest of the hardtack biscuit and bit off a bit of jerky. Chewing on this, he put the rest of what he had into his pockets and stood up. He started to walk, but he had no idea in which direction he was going.

Struggling through trees and underbrush, he stopped often to listen for sounds that might tell him if there were people around. Once he thought he heard shooting, but he couldn't tell whether it was real or whether he imagined it, so he hurried on. Soon the sound faded.

Finally, when the rays of the afternoon sun slanted through the shimmering leaves overhead, he came to a clearing. In the center was a small cabin made of weathered logs with dried mud filling the cracks between the logs. There were no windows, and the door stood ajar. Out back, a gray barn sagged in a tired way.

Josh circled the clearing from the safety of the forest, looking for signs of life. No smoke came from the chimney, no chickens scratched in the yard. There was no laundry hanging outside nor movement inside. It reminded him of the slave cabins near Fort Ellsworth, and he wondered whether there were slaves inside.

At dusk, he took off his army jacket and uniform shirt and buried them, careful to cover up the gold buttons. Standing in his undershirt, enjoying the cool evening air on his skin, he fidgeted with his suspenders, tightening them, snapping them softly against his stomach, all the time watching the house.

When he decided it was safe, he moved out of the woods toward the house, listening for a voice or the bark of a dog or a shot. He crossed the creaky porch, avoiding places where the rotting wood had been broken through, and pushed the door, which protested noisily on its hinges.

Inside, there were a few cracked dishes and a dented coffeepot on a dusty table. Beside the table, a chair lay on its side, as though its occupant had fled in haste.

In one corner was a wooden bed with a lumpy mattress. A crumpled rag doll lay on its back beside the bed, its black button eyes staring blankly up at Josh.

The memory came to him again. Happy faces around the table. Mattie, just a baby, clutching her rag doll. His mother, smiling, turning from the stove with a bowl in her hand. And then the memory was gone and he could not call it back. Picking up the doll, he smoothed its dress and, laying it carefully on the mattress, he left the house.

Around back was a small kitchen garden with a bent shovel lying among the weeds. Josh dug up the few remaining onions and potatoes and some round, red beets. He could feel saliva puckering his mouth.

Maybe the people who lived here had left a chicken behind when they fled. He hurried to the barn and tugged the door open. Inside, he was enveloped in the sweet-awful smell of hay and horse dung, an odor that reminded him of The Man's whiskey jugs. He wondered whether this farmer had hidden jugs under piles of straw.

Seeing that there were no animals in the barn, he turned to leave.

On a peg by the door hung a dirty, brown wool coat, tattered and patched and the patches tattered. Taking the coat down, he put it on to cover his undershirt. The sleeves hung several inches below his fingertips, and the bottom covered his knees. There was only one button, and the smell of sweat was strong and unpleasant. But now he didn't look like a deserter. Now he could start back home.

Josh returned to the place where he had buried his army clothes and dug them up. Removing everything from the pockets, he put it all in the pockets of his "new" coat. Then he put on his army shirt against the cool evening air and stood, trying to get the feel of where he was, the sense of which way was north.

The war is behind me, he decided. Tucking the smelly coat under his arm, he started into the darkening forest. He kept stumbling and falling down, so finally he wrapped himself in the coat and rested. The smell of sweat kept him awake for a while, but eventually the whispering trees lulled him to sleep.

When he awoke, the sun was high. Flies buzzed and landed on his face. Birds chattered in the trees overhead, and somewhere water was running. He followed the water sound, coming to wild berry bushes that tore at the heavy coat. He searched for berries, but there were none. Too early. There were only tiny white flowers among the thorns.

Taking off his boots, he squished through the soft, boggy ground toward the stream, soothing his feet in rich, cool mud. At the edge of the stream, clear water bubbled around boulders and swirled in shallow, stony pools.

Taking off all his clothes, he piled them on a dry rock and stepped into the stream. He lay down in the cold water, letting it run over the top of his head and into his mouth, drinking deeply. Sitting up, he scrubbed his face and body, and massaged his feet. He lay back down and looked at the sun-filled sky through a green canopy of leaves and branches, and was surprised that he felt happy.

He thought of Jere and found that the guilt was gone. I couldn't have helped him, he decided. I couldn't have kept the Rebs away. Jere was where he wanted to be, and he was happy.

A fish brushed against his leg and darted away. He thought of the first time Jere had taken him fishing, when he was six. How unexpectedly patient Jere had been, baiting his hook and showing him how to cast his line into a deep pool. "Now go and lie back from the edge of the river, so the fish won't see you," Jere had told him. Josh caught a big catfish that day and bragged that he had caught it by himself. Jere had let him have all the credit.

I'll try fishing toward evening, he thought. There are sure to be catfish here, too. With a sigh, he rose up out of the water, returned to his pile of clothing, and dressed.

He cleared away the brush and dug a hollow place, which he lined with stones. He gathered dry branches and built a small fire, using three of his matches. That left twenty in the box Hastings had given him. I'll have to be more careful, he thought.

The vegetables smelled like sweat when he removed them from the coat pockets. Well, boiling will get rid of that.

"Fool! You fool!" he cried out loud. "How can you boil vegetables without anything to put water in? You fool! Why didn't you bring that old coffeepot from the house?" His voice sounded harsh in the trees, like a tin cup banging on a tin plate. "How are you going to survive if you can't think any better than that?"

Can I find my way back to the log house, he wondered. No, I have to keep going on, not back. I don't want to go back anywhere. Not to the log house or the army or the war. I just want to go home. Feeling uneasy, he wondered where his home was.

He sat staring at the pile of vegetables for a while and remembered the sweet potato he had cooked for Jere back near Acquia Creek. He picked up a potato, two beets, and an onion and went back to the stream to scrub them. Then he poked them into his fire with a stick. While he waited for them to bake, he used his pocket knife to whittle a fork and then set to work carving a fish hook. He made it sturdy, gouging a hole in one end, and he threaded the hook with a boot lace, tying the lace to a long stick. So I can lie back from the edge of the water, as Jere said, he thought.

When he had finished these preparations, he ate his vegetables, which were sweet and smoky flavored. He couldn't taste the sweat.

Adding some wood to the fire, he rested until evening and then went back to the stream to fish. He put a piece of taffy on the hook as bait and lay on a large, flat rock, letting his hook rest on the bottom of a stony pool. In a few minutes, a whiskered catfish drifted by and grabbed the bait. Josh gave the line a jerk to set the hook and flipped the fish back onto dry ground. He removed the hook and tried again, catching two more fish before it grew too dark to see into the water.

Returning to his fire, he stirred it up and added more dry branches. Then he set to work cleaning the fish with his knife. He sliced off two large pieces from the sides of each fish. Wrapping these in damp leaves, he poked them into the rocks below the embers. If I cook these long enough, he thought, I'll have fish jerky that won't spoil on the trip north. He speared the bony parts of the fish with his long wooden fork and cooked them, eating them while they were still so hot they burned his mouth.

By this time it was dark, but Josh could not find the North Star in the cloudy sky. He decided to stay where he was, by the fire, for the night. He would write Mattie about Jere's death, while it was still fresh in his mind. He couldn't mail it, of course, but he would take it home to her.

He lit his little piece of candle from the dying fire and drew out a piece of Wycoff's paper and his pencil.

somewhere in the
Wilderness

Dear Mattie,

As I begin this letter, I am filled with sadness and more than a little worry. I do not know how you will receive the news that one of your brothers is dead, and the other is a deserter. Perhaps you have already seen Jere's name on the casualty lists. If I am captured, either by the Confederates or by our own soldiers, I will ask that this letter be sent on to you. You do not need to feel ashamed of your brother, Jere. He died a soldier's death, and it was over quick. As for whether you are ashamed of me, only you can decide that. I pray that you will not be.

The enemy attacked our camp. Jere was sitting by the fire cleaning his musket when the shooting began. He and his friend Mac were shot in the first volley. Jere was happy in the army. He had a good friend beside him when he died, and they were laughing.

Does that make it easier or sadder or harder to bear?

As for me, I don't know what I can say that will explain why I have run away from the army. It isn't fear because I do not believe I am afraid to die. I ran away because I could not stand the sight and sound of the killing. I decided not to go back because I am not sure whether the reasons people give for fighting are good enough to kill for or die for. I wish that there were some other choice that I could make so that I would not bring the shame of desertion to our family name.

Please do not blame me for not taking care of Jere. I did try, but in the end I just couldn't. I want to come home, so you will not be alone and so I will not be alone either. If I did not have you . . .

Josh stopped writing. *What would I do if I did not have Mattie? What else can I write to her? That I saw a rag doll yesterday and it reminded me of her? That I bathed naked in a stream and felt happy at the sight of the blue sky and the feel of cool water and the warm sun?*

He decided to finish the letter later. Wrapping himself in the smelly coat, he lay down and slept.

The next morning, he took the cooked fish out of the coals and opened up the leaves, which were charred and stuck to the fish. He was disappointed because the fish was not tough, like jerky, but still soft. He tasted some and spat it out with a snort. He took another bite and decided, well, it was food, and so he ate some more.

Then he wrapped the rest in leaves and put it in the coat pocket. *Maybe the sweat smell will flavor it,* he thought, laughing at the unpleasant idea. His laugh was harsh in the stillness.

Rolling the coat into a tight pack, he tied it to the end of his fishing pole, and, putting the pole over his shoulder, walked into the hot, steamy day.

After several hours, he came to faint wagon tracks that skirted the forest. He followed the shallow ruts until they were joined by another set. It was easier to follow them now. The woods thinned and became fields. Up ahead, the tracks met a road. He didn't see anyone on the road, but he decided to lie low until dark.

Resting in the cool of the trees, he took out a sheet of paper and began to write without thinking, really, just letting the words fill the paper.

> I am going to write down what I am thinking because it is very lonely just talking to myself, with only the trees to hear me. Maybe it will help me get through the days alone if I write down my thoughts.
>
> I wrote Mattie once that there was a lot I did not know. I realize now that there is even more I do not know than I ever imagined back on the road to Fredericksburg. I don't really know very much about myself. Being alone I find I think more and more about myself and wonder why I am the way I am. Why am I so serious? I used to wish I could be more like Jere, happy all the time, and jolly. I think maybe he deserved to live more than I because he enjoyed living so much. But he died, and I am the one who is alive.
>
> I don't know what purpose my life has, but I would like to do something really good with it. Only I don't know how to start. Perhaps being a deserter will make it hard for me to make my life mean something, but it's too late to go back now, and I don't believe I should. I could not put another man's face in my sights and pull the trigger. How could I do that after seeing what happened to Jere and Mac?
>
> There was a time yesterday when I felt happy, but I do not feel happy now. I feel terribly alone and wonder what is ahead for me. It is almost dark enough for me to see the stars. After I eat, I'll go back to the road and see if I can find the North Star. If no disaster befalls me, I'll write more another time.

When Josh returned to the road, he found the North Star just above where the road disappeared into the darkness. The Dipper was there, too, the drinking gourd. He wondered whether the Negro man and the boy were looking at the stars, too.

"I'm like them," he whispered. "I hide during the day and travel at night. I'm a deserter, but what is their crime? The color of their skin? Is that why they have to hide?"

He traveled for several nights, resting and writing during the day.

> Jere wanted to be a soldier so badly, but he
> never even fired his musket at the enemy. Perhaps
> he was lucky. Maybe killing wouldn't have been
> such an adventure for him after all.
> I wonder what mother would have thought
> about all this. Would she have thought killing was
> right when you are fighting for something you be-
> lieve is right, as some say this war is right? Or
> would killing always be wrong? Could it be right
> for some, like Jere, but not for others, like me? How
> do you choose between two things when both are
> right? How do you choose between two things
> when both are wrong?

When the road Josh was following turned west toward the misty, blue mountains in the distance, he wrote,

> Are those the mountains Jere saw from the bal-
> loon? He said he saw mountains going all the way
> to the Potomac River, but I didn't believe him.
> Maybe if I follow those mountains, I'll be going
> north. It seems Jere is still showing me what to do.
> How strange the way my thoughts wander. Jere
> is dead, so how can he still be showing me what to
> do? Perhaps he always will. I still hear Mother,
> sometimes, telling me what to do. So why shouldn't
> Jere be showing me what to do?

Each day, he listened for the sounds of war. Finally, he decided he had left all that behind. He still traveled at night to avoid people, and when he saw a farm, he circled wide around it.

One day while he was resting in a shady grove of trees, a flock of wild turkeys flapped down from the branches overhead and landed in a nearby field, striding about on scrawny legs. Josh studied them for several minutes, wondering how he could get one. He searched noise-lessly until he found a sturdy Y-shaped stick. He took off his suspenders and knotted the ends around the arms of the stick. Filling his pockets with stones, he inched his way forward on his belly, closer, closer.

The turkeys didn't pay any attention to him. They scratched and pecked near a rotten log, clucking and gobbling as they ate. Hardly seeming to move, Josh pulled a large stone from his pocket and placed it in the middle of the suspender, pinching the rock delicately between his thumb and forefinger. Slowly he drew the suspender taut, pulling it farther and farther back. Then, as gently as if he were squeezing the trigger of the musket, he released his fingers. The rock swooshed forward and caught a scrawny Tom turkey on the side of the head, killing him instantly. The other turkeys fled, squawking and flapping, in a dozen directions, some fluttering into low tree branches, others jumping madly around in circles, feathers flying.

Josh slung the turkey over his shoulder and retreated to the trees. Using the last of his matches, he lighted a fire. While it burned down, he plucked and cleaned the turkey and cut chunks of breast meat from the bones. Wrapping the pieces in wet leaves, he poked them into the embers. He speared a drumstick with his fork, now blackened from use, and sat cross-legged by the fire, roasting the meat over the hot coals.

Tantalized by the smell of the cooking turkey, he removed the drumstick from the fork. Without waiting for it to cool, he bit into the tough meat, tearing at it with his teeth.

The meat tasted wild and strong. Like me, he thought.

By morning, the turkey had cooked through and shriveled up. He started north again, following the contour of the mountains until, early one morning, he reached the broad Potomac River. We crossed this river at Washington three months ago on our way to Fort Ellsworth, he mused. When I get across, I'll be almost home.

He had to travel along the river by day now because he was looking for a bridge or a narrows or some way across the swiftly moving water. He avoided the road, still worried that someone might see him. One afternoon, he rested in a clump of trees and watched some chickens scratching in the yard of a large stone farmhouse. A woman was hanging washing on a clothesline on the other side of the house. A child cried, and she went inside.

One of those plump chickens would surely taste good, he thought, his mouth watering. He searched his pockets for hardtack crumbs, but there were none left.

After a while, his eyes grew heavy watching the chickens, and he dozed.

"What have we here?" a voice behind him boomed.

★★ Ten ★★

THE MUTINEERS

"WHAT have we here?" Josh opened his eyes and stared stupidly at the man looming in front of him. "Who are you, boy? Why are you hiding?" the man asked roughly.

Scrambling to his feet, Josh saw another man, smaller, with red-brown hair and a fox-like face, pointed at the nose. Both men wore Union Army uniforms.

"Who are you, boy?" the big man repeated. Josh noticed gold sergeant's stripes on the man's sleeve and turned to run, but there were two more soldiers behind him.

Will they hang me? The idea twisted painfully in his stomach like hunger. Is there anything I can say? He had heard that the condemned get to say some last words. Looking closely at the soldiers, he realized they were not armed. What if I just run? But he saw there was no place to hide in the sparse woods. His head spun, and he sank to one knee.

"Here, boy, are you all right?" the fox-faced man asked.

"Who are you?" the big man insisted.

"I'm Joshua Parish, and I'm lost."

"Lost?" the big sergeant boomed.

"Lost?" the fox-faced man echoed, more gently.

"What do you mean, lost?" a man behind him asked.

The sergeant studied him. "That looks like an army shirt to me. Is the army taking little boys now?"

"I'm a drummer, but I lost my company."

"Lost your company! By Gar, that's a good one. Lost your company! Where did you lose it, boy?" the man behind him said, slapping his dusty hat on his dusty knee.

"Near the Rappahannock," Josh mumbled.

"You're a long ways from the Rappahannock, Joshua Parish," the sergeant told him.

"Yes, sir," Josh answered looking up into the sergeant's unsmiling eyes.

"When did you lose your company?"

"Where are you headed?"

"When did you eat last?"

"Yesterday morning. I ate my last food yesterday."

"We don't have much, but I have a piece of hardtack I've been saving. It got a little wet and moldy, but if you're hungry, you're welcome to it, Joshua Parish," the fox-faced man offered.

"Yes, please." Taking the biscuit, Josh bit off a big piece and handed it back. In his eagerness, he swallowed too soon, before it was paste in his mouth, and choked and sputtered. The sergeant thumped him on the back so hard he nearly knocked Josh over, and the other soldiers hooted.

"You men, hurry up," a rude voice called from the road.

"We're coming. We're coming. Hold your horses," the fox-faced man called back just as rudely.

"Who's that?" Josh asked, looking around the big man at a Union soldier standing in the middle of the road, a rifle in his hands.

"That's our jailer," the dusty man told him.

"Your jailer? Are you prisoners?" Josh blurted out in amazement.

"Well, we're not exactly prisoners. We're mutineers," the sergeant explained.

"What are mutineers?" Josh asked.

The men all spoke at once. "We just kind of refuse to do what we're told."

"They've got no right to keep us here."

"We should have been sent home with the rest of our regiment."

"We want what's right," the dusty man finished up.

"It's not as though we're deserters or anything like that," the fox-faced man said. Then, seeing Josh's stricken face, he added, "You're no deserter, boy. You're just lost." He guffawed with laughter, and the dusty soldier slapped his knee with his hat again and grinned.

"Well, Joshua, you better come along with us for a while," the sergeant decided. "At least you'll get to eat." Josh nodded. The four mutineers pushed Josh into the middle between them. Walking, all bunched up, they returned to the road.

The soldier with the rude voice and the rifle didn't bother to look

at them. He said crossly, "Move along, you men. We're already behind the others."

The four mutineers and the boy hurried up the dusty road, passed
the farmhouse with the chickens scratching in the yard, and soon
caught up with a larger group of soldiers shuffling up the road.

"We're from the Second Maine Volunteers," the sergeant told
Josh as they walked. "I'm Sergeant Wallace, and this is Martin," he
pointed to the dusty man. "And Charles Dee." The quiet man nodded
his head.

"We're from Bangor," Sergeant Wallace continued.

"I'm George Wigney." The fox-faced man extended his hand to
Josh. "From down along the coast."

Smiling, Josh shook hands with all of them. "I'm glad I found
you."

"Found us. He says he's glad he found us." George grinned a sly,
fox-like grin.

"First you were lost, and now you found us. Well, we're glad you
found us, too, Joshua Parish."

"Why do they say you're mutineers?" Josh wanted to know.

"Well, the rest of our regiment went on home last month when
their enlistment was up, but the army said we had to serve another
year," Sergeant Wallace explained.

"They tried to put us into a Pennsylvania regiment, but we refused to fight with strangers. We signed up to fight with Maine men,"
Martin continued the story.

"We'll fight with Maine men or not at all," George exclaimed,
loudly, so the guard could hear him.

"So now they call us mutineers."

"And try to starve us to make us give in."

"And threaten to shoot us."

"But we just want what's right."

"We're Maine men, and we'll fight with Maine men or not at all."
George repeated.

Josh realized that his new friends had accepted what he had told
them about himself. He wondered how they would feel about him if
they knew he had run away. He guessed he wouldn't tell them right
now. He'd march along with them wherever they were going, and
later he could slip away and follow the North Star to Rochester.

The mutineers, 120 of them, with Josh in their midst, crossed the
Potomac River on a wobbling pontoon bridge and marched north

under the prodding of their guards. Josh liked having company after being by himself for so long. He enjoyed the men's jokes and their rough language. They shared their food with him and told stories of the places they had been and of their families back home. Josh told them about Mattie and The Man and about Jere's death by the campfire. The mutineers said they were sorry about his brother and promised they would try to get him safely back to his sister in Rochester.

It was the last part of June and blistering hot marching in the sun. There was no shade along the roadside when they stopped. They had only hardtack to eat, but they drank and cooled their faces whenever they found a stream. Then, lying back in the grass, they rested.

"On your feet, men. We've found a home for you," the guard bellowed one morning. Angry, the mutineers sat still or turned away.

"On your feet, or I'll shoot you," the guard fumed. Grumbling, the mutineers dragged themselves up and gathered slowly on the dusty road. Some cursed; others were silent and sullen. When the guard prodded them, they shuffled along without talking. Toward dusk they halted. Up ahead on the road, the captain of the guards spoke to a tall officer with a droopy, brown mustache and somber eyes.

"You have permission to shoot 'em if they give you trouble, Colonel."

The colonel nodded and dismissed the captain. He came over to where the mutineers had slumped down in the grass. Speaking in a quiet way, he told them, "My name is Colonel Chamberlain. I'm commander of the Twentieth Maine." The mutineers did not look up.

"Our regiment had one thousand men when we left Maine a year ago. Now there are fewer than three hundred of us. I suppose we were like you and came to war for the same reasons—to save the Union or for adventure or glory or because we just didn't want to stay at home. Many of us came because we thought it was right to free the slaves."

The colonel continued more strongly, "You will have to come along with us now. I cannot treat you as guests, but I will treat you fairly, as soldiers should be treated. If you fight with us, we will be glad to have you. I'll put your names on our rolls, and you will be part of a Maine regiment again. Nothing more will be said about mutiny."

Now the men looked up, interested. Slowly George Wigney rose, and the big sergeant stood up with him. A trace of a smile crossed the colonel's face before he turned and walked toward his horse. He spoke briefly to a young lieutenant, then led his horse to the head of

90

the column and began to walk up the dusty road. One by one, the mutineers stood up and moved forward, following George Wigney and the sergeant. Josh caught up with Sergeant Wallace.

"You don't need to come, Joshua. I'll explain to the lieutenant how young you are, and you can stay back."

"I'll come with you, Sergeant." Josh said.

"All right, then, Joshua. It will be a privilege to have you with us." Josh and Sergeant Wallace started up the road side by side.

The Twentieth Maine regiment marched in the dark that night and all the next day. They had orders to meet General Meade's Fifth Corps in Pennsylvania to form a barrier between the advancing Confederate Army and the Union capital at Washington.

They marched up through Maryland and crossed into Pennsylvania on July 1, talking as they went.

"We can't be late."

"They say this will be the biggest battle of the war."

"We need to give 'Old Snapping Turtle' a hand."

People from the Pennsylvania farms and towns along the way waved flags and cheered as they passed. Young girls placed flower garlands around the soldiers' sunburned necks. A pretty girl handed Josh a loaf of bread, saying breathlessly, "I baked it just for you."

Blushing, Josh mumbled his thanks and shared the still-warm loaf with his comrades. Jere would have loved the pretty girl, he thought, and thanked her in a much friendlier way. Tears stung his face, making rivulets down his dusty cheeks. Still, he thought. I still have tears for Jere.

The column turned west at Hanover, into the afternoon sun, and stopped as it grew dark. Josh and the sergeant went to a small stream where almost three hundred other men were cooling themselves in the water, muddy now with so many bathers.

While they ate and rested, Josh found a quiet place a little apart from the others and took out the letter he had started to Mattie in the Wilderness.

> I feel I should come home, so you will not be
> alone and so I will not be alone either. If I did not
> have you—

"Are you reading a letter from home?" Colonel Chamberlain's voice cut suddenly into Josh's thoughts.

"No . . . No, sir, I'm . . . I'm . . . ," Josh stammered as he scrambled to his feet.

"Sit down, son," the colonel said, lowering himself down onto the grass beside Josh. Josh could feel his face blush beneath his sunburn. He had never spoken directly to an officer, except for Captain Hale, and he didn't know what to say to the colonel now that they were sitting side by side.

"My brother tells me you are from New York," the colonel continued.

"Your brother, sir?"

"Lieutenant Chamberlain. The adjutant. He's my brother."

Josh stared at the colonel, surprised he had a brother, surprised they were in the war together.

"Sergeant Wallace from the Second Maine told my brother, Lieutenant Chamberlain, that they found you wandering somewhere north of the Wilderness."

"Yes, sir."

"He said that you were a drummer from one of the New York regiments that was ambushed by Confederates near Chancellorsville. He said you were lost."

"Yes, sir."

"And that you are thirteen."

Josh nodded.

"And your name is Joshua, the same as mine."

"Your name is Joshua, sir?"

The colonel nodded. "Do you want to tell me about the ambush?" His voice was gentle, almost friendly.

Josh thought for a few minutes watching the colonel who sat patiently.

"Well, sir, I wasn't lost," Josh began. He spoke so softly the colonel had to lean forward to hear, his face serious.

"I ran away," Josh continued. Slowly, hesitantly, he told the colonel about Jere and the campfire and the Rebel yell. He told him about picking up the musket and swinging it into the first Rebel face he saw.

"I think I killed him. I felt his head smash when I hit him."

"Was he the one who had killed your brother?" the colonel asked.

"I don't know. I didn't see who shot Jere."

The colonel nodded. Josh told the colonel about running away and how he had survived and about the runaway slaves who had told

92

him about the drinking gourd. He told about Mattie and the letter he had been writing to her and how he had met the mutineers. Shy at first, he could not stop talking once he started. The colonel's blue eyes watched him closely.

When Josh stopped, he sat still, breathing heavily.

"I see," was all the colonel said. After a time, he continued, "You can put all that behind you, Joshua. I will enter your name along with the others on the roll of the Twentieth Maine. No one else ever needs to know what you have told me tonight."

A flood of relief washed over Josh and he struggled to speak. "Th . . . thank you, sir."

"When this battle up ahead is over, I will find a way to send you home."

"Home?"

"Tomorrow during the battle we'll find something for you to do behind the lines."

"Please, sir, I would like to stay with the other men, the mutineers," Josh interrupted.

"You're only thirteen, Joshua. This war does not require a boy of thirteen to fight as a soldier. There is other work that you can do."

"Please, sir, I want to stay with the mutineers," Josh insisted.

"Well, then, Joshua, that is what you shall do." The colonel stood up. His shoulders sagged, but he straightened them. "When you have finished your letter to your sister, give it to the adjutant. He'll see it gets sent off. She is sure to be worried about you." Turning, he walked away.

Josh stared at the letter in his hand, trying to focus his mind on the words. Finally, he picked up his pencil and resumed writing.

> If I did not have you, dear Sister, I would proba-
> bly have found some place to hide until I was either
> caught or grown too old for anyone to care what I
> had done. But now, if I can find some way to avoid
> disgracing you and our family name, I will do it.
>
> It is some weeks since I started this letter. I
> have joined a regiment of soldiers from Maine who
> are headed for a battle in the farmlands of Pennsyl-
> vania. I do not know what I will do when I am faced
> with killing, but I will march with these soldiers
> and do my duty as best as I can.

I must close my letter now. The colonel who
commands this regiment says I must send it off to
you tonight so that you will not be anxious any
longer about your loving brother,

Josh

Josh folded the letter, addressed it, and gave it to the young lieutenant. A few moments later a soldier on horseback approached from
the west, riding at full gallop, churning up dust as he came. Sliding
off his lathered horse, he spoke excitedly to the colonel. A bugler
blared the call to march.

Weary soldiers dragged themselves to their feet and formed a column on the road. Word passed down the line. "We must get to Gettysburg before dawn."

"Where?"

"To Gettysburg."

"That way, another twenty miles."

"Well, then, let's get moving."

The drummer began a steady marching beat. Josh hurried to take
his place between George Wigney and Sergeant Wallace, and they
started west on the dark road to Gettysburg.

✯✯ *Eleven* ✯✯

GETTYSBURG

T HE soldiers marched in the moonlight past rail fences and stone
farms. When clouds hid the moon, they shuffled along in darkness, stumbling, unable to see anything except the men in front of
them.

Long after midnight, they stopped east of the sleeping town of
Gettysburg. Josh staggered into a field beside the road and fell asleep,
the cool grass cradling his body.

When he opened his eyes it was day, and he could see the bodies
of soldiers all around him, sleeping where they had fallen the night
before. Sitting up, shaking himself awake, he looked out over the valley in front of him. Soft gold wheat grew to the edge of the woods,
where bright yellow wildflowers splashed against the dark trees. In
the distance, misty mountains rose blue-gray against the morning sky.
It was still, this time just after dawn.

Exhausted, he lay back down and slept again, waking at midday
to the sound of gunfire in the distance. Around him the others woke
up, too. Stretching, talking, they searched for food in their pockets
and packs. Hardtack was all they found. They straggled up to the
road, toward the smell of coffee brewing, and returned with steam-
ing mugs in which to soak their hard biscuits. When they had eaten,
they lay back down in the tall grass, some dozing, others talking
quietly.

"The colonel's coming," shouted the sergeant of the regiment.
The soldiers lying in the field stood up, drew together, and watched
the tall, spare figure of Colonel Chamberlain approach.

"We have arrived here in time. Up ahead, beyond the town, there
is a battle raging. We will be called upon to fight." Looking at the
mutineers, he went on. "We can use any who will fight with us today.

95

"This is now the third summer of the war, and today may be the most important battle of all. If we cannot hold here, nothing will stop the Confederates from going on to capture our capital at Washington."

The men stirred restlessly.

"Do you see that hill up there?" The colonel pointed to a small hill covered with boulders and trees. "There is no one on that hill right now, but if the Confederates take it, they will climb right up and drive our forces from the top of that ridge where you see our cannon firing." Josh saw the puffs of artillery fire hanging on the still air and, nearby, the Stars and Stripes above the trees.

"Does the little hill have a name, sir?"

"Well, the big one next to it is called Big Round Top."

"Why not Little Round Top, then?" The others agreed.

"Maine will be proud of you, her sons, for what you do today." The colonel turned and walked quickly back to where his brother waited on the road.

The regiment formed and started for Little Round Top. Scrambling up the rocky slopes, they took a position where they could look down into the valley through the shimmering leaves of oak and maple trees. Great, gray boulders jutted out from the damp leaves and rocks that covered the ground. A squirrel flicked its bushy tail and scampered up a tall hickory-nut tree to hide in the leaves near the top.

"We must hold this left side of the line at all costs. If the Confederates break through here, they'll sweep on up the hill and around behind us." The soldiers listened to the colonel and understood what they must do.

"All right, spread out. Build yourselves breastworks for protection and pile the stones high. That will make it harder for the enemy to climb over." Experienced soldiers, the men did not need to be told what to do, but they were reassured as the colonel moved among them, speaking with some, encouraging others.

The line spread out more than a hundred feet on either side of Josh. Some men crouched behind trees, others built rock barricades. Josh and a boy Jere's age helped Sergeant Wallace fill the gap between two trees.

"Joshua Parish," a voice called from above. "The adjutant wants to see you up here."

Josh hesitated, looked around. "Up you go," Sergeant Wallace said. "We'll finish here."

"Why? What does he need me for?"

"That's not for you to question, Joshua. Now be off with you," the sergeant warned.

Muttering, shaking his head, Josh climbed the rocky hill to where Lieutenant Chamberlain waited.

"You wanted me, sir?" Josh asked.

"Yes, Joshua. This message has to go over to Colonel Vincent. There." He pointed farther along the little hill.

"But, sir, I was helping . . . " Josh stopped and looked helplessly at Colonel Chamberlain several feet away talking with the regimental sergeant. The colonel ignored him.

"I need you *now.* You're small and quick, and you can get there faster than any of the others. Go!" The lieutenant thrust a folded paper at Josh.

With a glance downhill at Sergeant Wallace, Josh turned and scrambled across the rocks to find Colonel Vincent and hand his staff officer the message.

"Wait for a reply." The officer turned away abruptly.

As Josh waited, cannon began to fire. He was surrounded by the resonant *boom, boom* of cannon to his right, the *pop, pop, pop* of muskets below, the faint *boom* of cannon across the valley on the Confederate side. Cries of, "Here they come!" "Come on!" "Look there!" reached him. In the valley below, Josh saw the dust of marching soldiers, coming closer, coming up the hill. The sun shone on the metal of musket barrels and bayonets. The firing increased.

Had they forgotten him? Starting back to the Twentieth Maine, he saw two men carrying Sergeant Wallace up the hill. Blood gushed from a tear in the sergeant's shoulder. Shreds of skin and muscle hung from the gaping wound.

"You got a doctor up here?" one man shouted. It was the dusty soldier, Martin.

"Over yonder," a voice answered.

Josh helped them move Sergeant Wallace nearer the doctor. Then the others slipped back down the hill into the battle, leaving Josh to remove the sergeant's coat and tear away his shirt. He was holding the sergeant's torn shirt over his wound to keep some of the blood from spilling out when the doctor came.

"Good lad," the doctor said quickly and poured water from a canteen onto the wound. The sergeant muffled a scream with his fist.

"You're lucky. The bullet passed clear through." The doctor covered the wound with a big wad of bandage. "Here," he shoved the roll of bandage at Josh. "Press hard on the wound until it stops bleeding, then wrap it up. You," the doctor spoke to the sergeant, "Rest here. You've lost a lot of blood," and the doctor was gone.

Josh pressed on the wound. The sergeant closed his eyes and gasped, "Come on, come on, boy. Wrap it up."

We wrapped and wrapped until my arms were sore, Mattie had written.

Josh wound the bandage up over the sergeant's torn shoulder, still shiny wet with blood. Down under his armpit and around his chest. Again and again until only a faint tinge of blood showed through the bandage.

"Help me with my coat, Joshua," Sergeant Wallace demanded as Josh tied the bandage.

"Are you cold?" Josh asked.

"No," the sergeant laughed. "But if I'm going back into that brawl, I'd best be wearing my blue coat, or my own boys might shoot me next time."

"You can't go back there," Josh cried. "The doctor told you to rest here."

"Of course I'm going back, boy. I'm needed there. Things are bad."

"You've lost too much blood. You're weak," Josh argued.

"Nonsense, Joshua, I'm as fit as the next man. Now help me with my coat." The sergeant held out his coat. "Come on!" he ordered, shaking the coat at Josh.

Taking the bloody coat, Josh managed to get the sergeant's good arm into a sleeve, easing it gently but causing the sergeant to bellow in pain. He tucked the empty sleeve into the side pocket and buttoned the coat across the sergeant's broad chest.

"There. Neat as a pin," Sergeant Wallace chuckled. "Now, help me down the hill." He clung to Josh with his good arm and they slid and stumbled down into the raging battle.

Josh lost sight of the sergeant in the smoke that hung on the hot afternoon air like a curtain, not quite hiding the horror of the battle, not quite covering the bodies. He could understand why the sergeant had said things were bad. Soldiers in blue uniforms and gray lay twisted together. Faces stared up at him, eyes wide, mouths open.

Josh searched for some way to help and spied Martin, who had brought Sergeant Wallace up the hill less than an hour ago. His wrist

98

was shattered, his face twisted with pain. Running to him, pulling, dragging, he got Martin up the hill.

"Good boy," Martin gasped, helping as best he could.

Josh stayed and helped the doctor, holding the wooden splint while the doctor wrapped it with a long roll of bandage, then another. "Here," the doctor said to Josh. "You finish it." Josh wrapped the splinted wrist until there was no more bandage left on the roll.

Martin insisted on going back.

"How will you shoot?" Josh asked as they made their way down the hill.

"You can load for me, and I'll pull the trigger with my other hand," Martin said. "We'll fight those Johnny Rebs together." He disappeared into the smoke calling, "Come on. Over here."

Another voice in the smoke shouted, "We have no more ammunition! Colonel, we need more ammunition!"

As Josh started after Martin, his foot slid out from under him. Looking down, he realized with horror that he had stepped on a body.

"I'm sorry," Josh gasped, dropping to his knees, but the man was dead and did not answer.

He crawled on all fours to the next wounded soldier. Cradling the man's head in his lap, he opened his canteen. "Here," he offered. "Drink."

A bullet struck the tree beside him with a dull *thud*. Another shot away a branch above his head, raining twigs and leaves down on him, but Josh hardly noticed the bullets and the noise and the danger all around. For an hour, more, he crawled among the wounded and the dying, climbing the hill to fill and refill his canteen and stumbling back down to hold it to parched lips. He poured water into his hand and bathed bleeding faces. He lifted and carried and dragged the wounded up the hill to the doctor. He wrapped and wrapped until his arms were sore.

Each time he went down into the battle, men crowded around him. "Is there more ammunition up there?"

"We have none."

"Even the dead have none any longer."

"Josh, we need more ammunition!"

"Lieutenant, we need more ammunition!"

"Colonel, we need more ammunition if we are to hold!"

"Ammunition!"

"Ammunition!"

99

The popping sound of muskets slowed as the Rebels fell back to regroup. Then, they came again. Above them, near the center of the line, the colonel raised his sword and shouted, "Bayonets!"

Surprised at first, the men took up the cry. "Bayonets!" They passed the word along sharply like the sound of steel bayonets hitting steel muskets.

"Bayonets fixed," the men returned the shout.

"Bayonets forward!" The colonel's voice filled the little hill, and the soldiers on the left side of the line began to move down the hill and to the right, toward the center, like a gate swinging forward on its hinge.

"Come on! Come on! Come on, boys!" an eager voice cried out.

"Here." A soldier passed Josh a musket and picked up another from the ground. Holding the musket in front of him, its long steel bayonet pointing toward the trees below, Josh moved down the hill, unsteady at first because the musket was so heavy. Suddenly in front of him, three Rebel soldiers threw their hands up in the air.

"We surrender!"

"We're your prisoners."

"Don't shoot us!"

Thunderstruck, Josh hooted, "I'm not going to shoot you. Move along ahead of me." With his bayonet pointing at their backs, he marched his captives up the hill.

"Good work, son," the sergeant in charge of prisoners told him. "Now go back and bring me some more."

By the time Josh got back down the hill, the battle was slowing. Confused and frightened, the Rebs either surrendered or retreated across the valley to the other side.

By six o'clock, the battle was over. Smoke hung heavy in the air as the light grew dim among the trees, and it was quiet, except for the sound of sobbing and the cries for help.

Josh moved among the dead and wounded, giving water, wrapping a wound with a torn shirt, speaking words of comfort. He came to George, the fox-faced man, and Martin, the dusty soldier. The two lay side by side, not moving.

They gave me their food when I had none, thought Josh. They were my friends. Do all the ones I care about have to die? Desperate, he looked around for Sergeant Wallace and was relieved to see him leaning against a tree, though his wounded shoulder was spewing blood again. In the distance he saw Colonel Chamberlain, limping as he passed among his troops.

Near the top of the next hill, a man sat on a large, flat rock, sketching the awful scene below him. "Wycoff!" Josh gasped, reaching out to steady himself on a tree.

The colonel's voice spoke beside him. "Are you wounded, Joshua?"

"No, sir, I'm not hurt."

"You served well today and perhaps saved many lives. I will say that in my report."

"Thank you, sir."

With a weary smile, the colonel told Josh, "Go up and see my brother. He has more work for you to do."

"Yes, sir."

Before starting up the hill, Josh looked again for Wycoff, but the artist was gone. He reported to the lieutenant and spent the next hours delivering messages. When he returned to his regiment, night had come, and the battlefield was quiet. Josh lay down with the others and slept among the dead.

★★ *Twelve* ★★

THE DAY AFTER

THE early morning sun shone pink through the thick smoke lingering over the valley. Near Josh, Sergeant Wallace stirred and sat up, bellowing, "Lordy, I'm hungry!" Around them, everyone laughed. They had all gone to sleep without eating.

The colonel came, still limping, to walk among the men, talking briefly with each one before moving on to the next.

"Splendid valor," he said to a bleeding man.

"What heroic souls!" he said to others.

Then, "We are going to move on," he said, pointing to a clump of oak trees on the next ridge over. "It's a nice safe place up there, the center of our line, where our cannon are. General Meade's headquarters are there, where all the flags are."

"They got any food?" Sergeant Wallace asked, and the others cheered.

"We will see if they do," the colonel nodded.

"And ammunition. We need more in case we do any more fighting." The men bantered pleasantly, their tension relieved by laughter.

"Yes, well, I think there will be food and ammunition up there." Turning to Sergeant Wallace, the colonel said, "I thank Providence for you men from the Second Maine. I do not think we could have held without you yesterday."

The sergeant spoke for the others. "It was an honor fighting with you, Colonel."

Leaving the wreckage of Little Round Top, Josh climbed with the others to their new position on Cemetery Ridge. There was food and hot coffee there.

"How about some cherry pie to go with that?" someone suggested.

"I'd like a tall drink of milk," Josh grinned.

The lieutenant called to Josh, explaining, "My runner has been mortally wounded, and I need another. Yesterday I saw how fast and quick-witted you are. Take this message to General Meade's aide." The lieutenant pointed to a small house some distance away, where officers clustered in small groups.

"There's a good lad," the lieutenant called after him. "Move quickly, now."

When Josh reached the small house, he handed the message to the general's aide and was told to wait for a reply. He sat down on a rocky ledge.

Looking out over the valley below, he saw a long sweep of field, a small orchard on the left, and a woods running from the valley up to the top of the ridge across from him. The Confederate camp.

Toward three o'clock, the Confederate cannon flashed, and puffs of smoke wreathed the big guns. In a few seconds, the sound reached Josh on the other side of the valley, a hollow *boom, boom.* A few guns at first, then all. From behind him, the Union cannon answered. Over and over cannon boomed and answered, and before long, the fields below were filled with smoke again.

Rolling off the ledge, Josh lay behind it where he could see what was happening in greater safety. Watching, listening, he felt as though it was all happening far away, in some other place, to another boy. He could see the other boy, himself, watching and listening.

Confederate soldiers came out of the woods across the valley, walking slowly at first, plodding forward across the fields and past the gray stone farms below. Small groups of men, thirty or fifty or a hundred, packed tightly together, their shoulders touching, their gray uniforms dusty. Above them, Confederate flags sagged in the breeze-less air.

The soldiers came forward until they filled the whole valley. Hundreds. Thousands. Above them, the Union cannon fired. With each boom, men in the valley below were thrown into the air or fell silently to the ground, but more came, marching with their muskets on their shoulders, their bayonets glinting in the smoky sunlight. It was hard to see the clusters of men anymore, but Josh could hear them yelling, cursing, crying out.

Up the hill in front of the approaching Confederate soldiers, the Union Army waited, hunched behind a stone wall, heads down, muskets ready.

As the first Confederate soldiers scrambled over a rail fence just

below him, Josh saw the Union soldiers rise up from behind the wall
and fire. A color sergeant raised the Stars and Stripes for all to see. He
fell to a bullet immediately, but the man beside him snatched the flag
and raised it high again.

The Confederates came, running now, firing, shouting. The Rebel
yell. Josh shuddered and saw the soldiers behind the wall shudder, too.

"Forward! Forward to the wall!" a Confederate officer commanded. He speared his wide hat on the tip of his sword and, holding
it high, he cried again, "Forward to the wall!" The men behind him
began to fall. First one by one, then four, then ten, like so many domi-
noes. Finally, the officer himself fell. With his sword piercing his hat,
he lay beside the wall.

In front of Josh a group of Zouave soldiers fired and reloaded, the
men's flashy red pantaloons and blue jackets with their rows of shiny
gold buttons catching the July sun. A young Zouave, shot in the leg,
struggled to stand and continue firing.

Josh inched forward on his stomach, pulling himself along with
his elbows, keeping his head down low to the dusty ground. Taking
the musket from the Zouave's hands, Josh removed the soldier's
bright blue coat and wrapped it tightly around the man's shattered leg.

How bravely they march, his mother had said when they pic-
nicked in the park. But this young soldier will never march bravely
again, Josh thought.

He pressed the wound with all his strength, and the man gasped
and fell beside him, behind the protection of the stone wall. When the
blood no longer oozed from beneath the coat, Josh moved on, through
the tangle of bodies, helping where he could.

An arm reached out to him. Josh looked into the blue eyes of a
boy, a little older than himself. Jere's age. Jere's eyes, blue and staring. But this boy wore gray and he was not dead. His hand clutched
Josh's arm.

"Water," the boy gasped.

Josh tore open his canteen and held it to the boy's mouth, gently
raising the bleeding head and letting water trickle into the open
mouth.

"Thank you," the mouth whispered. "Mother!" it cried.

What does he remember of his mother? Josh wondered. A happy
smile at the supper table? A promise given? The boy lay still. Josh
closed his lifeless eyes. I didn't do that for Jere. At least I can do it for
this Rebel soldier.

He dragged himself on. "I wish I knew how to do more," he said to one soldier. "I wish I could do more for you," he told another. "Thank you," a third man said before he died.

Finally, it grew quiet. Only one or two muskets still popped. In the fields, a riderless horse wandered through the field amid fallen flags and the broken bodies of men and animals. Wounded Union soldiers on stretchers were carried up over the ridge to the hospital. The dead were taken to a common resting place farther along the ridge.

Josh returned to his regiment and sat apart from the others, dazed, all the rest of the day. Have I seen hell? Why did I watch it? How could I not watch?

Sergeant Wallace came to sit beside him and offered him a fresh biscuit. Josh shook his head and turned away. After a while, the sergeant left.

Toward evening, Colonel Chamberlain came and sat with him but did not speak.

Breaking the silence, Josh asked, "Did you see it, sir? Did you see what happened in the valley?"

"I saw it, yes," the colonel answered sadly.

"How could you bear to see it, sir?" Josh asked fiercely. "How will you ever forget?" Turning, his stricken eyes, he searched the colonel's face.

"We shall never forget what we have seen today, Joshua. Not you nor I nor any one of us here. This place will never be the same, just as you and I will never be the same."

"You're right. I will never be the same." Josh spoke slowly, with long pauses, and the colonel did not interrupt. "I thought what happened to Jere was the worst that could happen to me, but it wasn't. This thing, today, the killing, it was worse. It keeps getting worse.

"There were so many. Not just us, but all of them." His voice trembled. "I know they are the enemy, but they are just like us. They look like us. They talk like us. They bleed like us. How does it make it right to say they are the enemy and shoot them?"

Josh waited. He wanted to scream at the colonel, "Say something that will make it all right."

When the colonel finally spoke, he said, "I don't know how to answer your question."

Disappointed, Josh cried bitterly, "Jere thought this war was going to be an adventure. He thought it would be all flags and marching and glory."

"Some men do think war is an adventure," the colonel admitted.

"They couldn't think of it as an adventure today." Pausing for breath, he continued vehemently, "I saw men who were enjoying it. They enjoyed the killing."

"I don't think many men enjoy killing, Joshua. Perhaps a few, but not many."

"They looked like they were enjoying it," Josh argued. "They looked pleased with themselves."

"Perhaps they were pleased that they were not being killed. In battle, men are pleased just to stay alive. They kill in order to keep from being killed."

When Josh did not respond, the colonel continued, "Most men here came to war because they thought it was the right thing to do. Many believed that freeing the slaves was right. Others came to preserve the Union. Now that they are here, they fight and kill in order to keep from being killed. That is how I think of it."

"Do you think killing is right? Is that what you mean?"

"Killing is a part of war, Joshua. It is not what we would choose, but it is what we must do when we fight for something we believe is right."

"And you think this war is right? Is that it, sir?"

"I believe so, yes, Joshua. But it is not enough for *me* to believe that it is right. That is not enough for you. You have to know what *you* believe."

"But that's just it, sir, I *don't* know. I don't know what I believe." Josh's voice sounded high in his ears.

"The day before yesterday when I said that you could stay behind the lines, why did you refuse?" the colonel asked.

Josh thought before he answered. "Well, partly because I wanted to help the men who had found me."

The colonel nodded.

"And partly because I wanted to do my part, to make up for running away."

"There are many ways to do your part, Joshua. I think you have found a good way—helping others. If each one of us does his part, we are each stronger. And we are stronger all together."

Calmer, breathing more easily, Josh went on, "After today, I know that killing isn't just a word. It isn't something you do and then just walk away. When you kill someone, he doesn't just get up and walk away either. He can't go home. If he's lucky, he gets buried in a grave. Killing is real. It's bloody, it's dead, it's forever. Do you see that?"

"Yes, Joshua, I do see that."

"Sometimes today I thought about the man and the little boy, the ones I told you about. They shouldn't have to run away just because they're black. I think that a man has the right to have black skin and not be afraid, don't you?"

The colonel nodded. "There is no simple answer, is there? Not for any of us, I'm afraid."

Josh and the colonel did not say anything more, but sat side by side for a while before they went back to camp.

The next day, July 4, both armies gathered up their dead and waited for the battle to begin again. Toward noon, Josh saw Wycoff sitting on a tree stump, sketching; the boy went to him, wondering how Wycoff would treat him.

When he saw Josh, Wycoff leaped up, dropping his paper and pencil, and hugged and pummeled him. "We thought you must be dead," he repeated over and over. "We gave you up for dead."

Josh told about wandering in the Wilderness, losing his way, and, finally, about meeting the mutineers. He did not lie about what had happened to him.

"Lucky for you," Wycoff kept saying. "Lucky thing they found you. Lucky you weren't killed in the ambush back in Virginia."

"And Jere?" Josh hesitated, wanting to know but afraid to ask.

"We buried him and MacNaughton in the same grave," Wycoff said. "There were so many graves to dig, more than half the company. Those two were always larking around together, so we just put them in the same grave."

Josh nodded. He was glad to know that Jere was not alone in his grave.

"I'll draw you a picture of where he's buried," Wycoff said. "There's an old hollow oak and a small dogwood tree there. The white flowers from the dogwood fall on the grave. When this war is over, you can go back and find the grave, you and your sister. I wrote her and told her that I hoped you were still alive, and I sent her back her letters."

"I'm obliged to you," Josh said.

Wycoff reached into his pocket. "I took this from Jere before we buried him." He handed Josh his father's watch. "See, here, this is where the bullet nicked it, but it still runs. I've kept it wound, and it still runs."

"Thank you."

"And your knapsack. You said it was your father's. I have it back in camp. Walk back with me and I'll give it to you."

Walking toward the New York regiment, Josh explained that he was now part of a new regiment, the Twentieth Maine.

"You were the ones that held Little Round Top, then," Wycoff said. "Captain Hale was wounded. He's in hospital down there. Sergeant Willard has gone down to see him." Wycoff pointed to the stone farm below them, behind the ridge.

"What about Eddie Boy?"

"Killed trying to protect the flag, right after your brother was shot," Wycoff said.

"I wonder whether he ever found out what a secessionist is?"

"What?"

"Never mind. What about Ruggles?" Josh asked. "Is he dead, too?"

"He's too ornery to get himself killed. He got shot up pretty bad in the ambush, but he's back and fighting now, mean as ever." Wycoff chuckled.

"Doesn't seem fair, does it? A sour apple like him, and he's still alive."

"War is sometimes a little short on fairness." Wycoff pointed up the hill. "He's up there, identifying the dead from our little company."

Josh saw Ruggles, shirt sleeves rolled up, turning bodies, staring.

"Come and say 'Hello,' " Wycoff suggested.

"Another time." Josh hoisted the knapsack onto his shoulder, shook hands with Wycoff, and returned to his regiment.

That night, even though he was bone-weary, he wrote to Mattie, hoping it would ease his mind to put his feelings down on paper.

Gettysburg, Pennsylvania
July 4, 1863

My Dear Sister,
    The campfire is lit and we are clustered around
it, but no one is singing. Our songs would be too
sad tonight. We have finished two days of terrible

fighting. I will not offend you by describing the battle or the ghastly destruction all around me now. I shall never forget it.

I have seen enough men killed in these last two days to fill the whole city of Rochester, all the shops and offices, all the parks and streets and houses. After today, I do not believe that I could kill even if my life depended on it. I pray that I will not have to make that choice.

I seem to have found a way to do my part without killing. My friend, Colonel Chamberlain, told me that by each of us doing our part we are able to do more than any one of us could do alone. He talks like that, as though he were reading from the Bible. He says I should be proud of my service helping the wounded. He is a kind man, so I think it must be hard for him to see so many die, but he is an officer so, of course, his men look up to him, and he must lead them into battle.

The colonel told me that I must decide for myself what I am to do. His brother, the adjutant, has asked me to be his runner, which I will do, glad to make myself useful in this way.

This morning I had the good fortune to see Wycoff from our old New York company. He described to me where Jere is buried and drew me a map so that when this war is over you and I can go there. He told me that he had written to you to tell you about Jere and to say that I might be alive. He said that he sent you back the letters you had written. I think that you should save the letters, Mattie, yours and all the ones I have written, such as they are. I believe it is important to remember all that happens in this war. Perhaps if we remember there will not need to be another like it.

I hope that I shall have a letter from you soon and that you will tell me how you are and give me news of Aunt Carrie and Uncle. You can tell me about the books you have read and how you pass the time when you are not in school. It will be

pleasant to hear of things other than war. Tell me
whether you have ever seen The Man and whether
he was angry because Jere broke his whiskey jugs.
Please write soon, your brother,

Josh

That evening, General Lee began the Confederate retreat back to
Virginia. From high on Cemetery Ridge, Josh saw that wherever
General Lee rode, Confederate soldiers reached out to touch him,
called his name, and cheered him as they wept. How can they cheer
him? He sent them into such a slaughter. Why do they still cheer?

Three days later, on July 7, the Army of the Potomac left Gettysburg to follow the Confederates back to Virginia, back to the Wilderness and the Rappahannock. Josh went with them.

Thirteen

THE SHADOW
OF DEATH

Rochester, New York
July 20, 1863

My Dear Brother,

You are alive! I am so happy to hear from you and to know that you are safe. When word reached us that Jere had been killed, we thought you might have been killed, too. Thinking that both my brothers were dead, as well as my parents, I became ill and could not eat. I just lay in bed and cried. Aunt Carrie nursed me so tenderly that I finally recovered. Uncle went each day to read the list of casualties downtown. After a while, when your name was not on any list, the recruiter said that you must be either wounded in a hospital somewhere or taken prisoner. You cannot imagine our relief when we finally received your letter telling us that you had been wandering in the woods, lost, all that time.

I recently had a kind letter from Mr. Wycoff telling me where Jere was buried. He said he would call on us when he returned to Rochester and would bring us Jere's things.

I have had two letters from you now, one you started while you were lost and the other written after the battle at Gettysburg. We have read accounts in the newspaper of the terrible losses to

both sides in that battle, so I can understand why
you were filled with such horror. I am glad you
have found something to do besides killing. Uncle
says that often serving as a runner or caring for the
wounded can be more dangerous than if you were
carrying a musket. He is very proud of you. Please
be careful and take no risks. I could not bear to lose
both of my brothers.

You asked me to save your letters. I have done
so from the very first one you sent from Fort
Ellsworth. Uncle has given me a cherrywood box
that I keep beside my bed, and I have filled it with
your letters and the story you told me when we
were still on the farm. It soothes me to read them
before I snuff out my candle and go to sleep.

We have heard nothing from The Man, but
friends who have passed by that way say that he has
married again, a widow with three sons. Perhaps
that will content him.

Would you like me to send you some books,
perhaps some adventure stories and a small Bible?
Do you have time to read when you are not busy?

My thoughts keep tumbling out onto the paper,
and I apologize for any errors. I pray for your safe
return and remain your loving sister,

Mattie

Around the little camp, his comrades dozed or cleaned their muskets, talking quietly. Some were playing cards. Josh sighed deeply.

Sergeant Wallace looked up with a worried frown. "Bad news
from home?"

"No," Josh answered searching for his paper and pencil. Maybe
if he wrote Mattie he would feel less lonesome.

near the Rappahannock again
August 15, 1863

Dear Mattie,

As happy as you were to have my letter, I was
happy to have yours and to know that you do not
blame me for Jere's death and are not ashamed of me

for deserting. I am sorry you were ill, and am grateful to Aunt Carrie for nursing you back to health.

As you can see, I am in the same place I was three months ago. The days are often tedious as we wait for something to happen, and I would be glad if you would send me books to read. Yes, I would like a Bible and maybe books about real things like the trees and birds. You can send adventure stories, too, though there is already too much adventure here.

I am sending you some pages that I wrote when I was lost in the Wilderness and put away in the bottom of my knapsack before the battle at Gettysburg. I am not embarrassed to have you read them. I think you will not laugh at me. At the time, I was very undecided as to my feelings about the war and my part in it. Now I believe that I am doing the right thing for me.

Please write again soon.

Your loving brother,

Joshua

As August passed into September, a deadly game of tag was played by the soldiers of both armies. One side would emerge suddenly from the woods, and there would be a battle. Then the soldiers would disappear into the trees, only to appear somewhere else the next day. And with each battle, five or ten or a hundred more were killed or wounded.

Early one morning, Colonel Chamberlain sent Josh with a message for General Meade.

"Keep your eyes open," Sergeant Wallace warned. "There are Rebel and Yankee renegades everywhere in the woods."

Josh smiled. They treat me like a child. I've been taking messages long enough to watch out for myself. Stuffing some jerky into his pocket to eat along the way, he slipped out of camp in the direction of headquarters.

Crossing a stony creek, he paused to pick some tart blackberries from the thorny branches that tore at his legs—just as they tore at me before, he thought . . . The hair on the back of his neck stood straight up. He saw the remnants of a campfire in the clearing where he stood, and a hollow oak, and a dogwood tree, heavy with red berries now instead of flowers. With a pounding heart, he dropped to his knees, clawing at the leaves, looking for Jere's grave.

A cold, hard voice cut across his consciousness. "Put your hands up over your head, boy." He steadied himself on the ground, turning slowly on all fours to face a disheveled soldier in a ragged uniform. Sergeant Wallace had warned him, but he had been too lost in his own eager search to heed the warning.

"Where's your musket?" The soldier stepped nearer, leveling his own musket at Josh's head.

Drawing a deep breath to calm himself, Josh answered, "I'm looking for my brother's grave. I don't have a gun."

"Got any food?"

Josh reached in his pocket and pulled out the jerky, which he tossed to the man.

Snatching the food, the renegade dropped his musket. He squatted across from Josh, filling his mouth and chewing noisily.

"Ain't you going to pick that up and shoot me?" he challenged, nodding toward the musket lying between them.

Struggling to keep his voice from trembling, Josh answered, "No."

"Not even if I tell you I'll shoot you soon's I finish eating?"

"Not even then."

Puzzled, the man frowned, then went back to eating. Josh tensed his muscles and lunged across the space between them. Seizing the musket by the barrel, he flung it as far as he could into the woods. Branches cracked, sending a shudder through the trees. Plunging across the creek, he stopped on the other side to look back. The renegade soldier stood, hands on his hips, shaking his head.

"Dang you, boy. It'll take me an hour to find my musket."

"I'll be long gone by then," Josh called out as he turned and ran. Behind him he heard the soldier cursing, "Dang you, boy, it wasn't even loaded."

Josh hooted with laughter and kept running.

In October, he received a package of books. Mattie sent him a small, leather-bound Bible and *The Knowledge of Nature,* about plants and animals and birds. Uncle sent a new scientific adventure story, *Five Weeks in a Balloon* by Jules Verne. Aunt Carrie put in a thick volume by Charles and Mary Lamb, the stories of William Shakespeare. The books helped him fill long hours when there was nothing to do but wait for the fighting to start again.

In November, Mattie sent him a copy of *The Democrat* with two sketches by Wycoff and a photograph of President Lincoln at the dedication of a national cemetery at Gettysburg. There was the text of the president's Gettysburg Address and a list of casualties from Rochester, killed in those three terrible days of fighting.

With a sad heart, Josh sat that evening searching through the little Bible that Mattie had sent. Colonel Chamberlain came by with his brother on their nightly rounds and stopped beside him.

"Do you need me, sir?"

"No, Joshua. I just wanted to see what you were reading."

"The Bible, sir."

The colonel's eyebrows shot up.

"I'm looking for a psalm I used to read to my mother when she was sick. She said it comforted her. Something about the valley of death," Josh explained.

"Look at the Twenty-third Psalm," the colonel suggested.

Josh thumbed the pages until he found it. "This is the one, sir. How did you know? Have you read it?"

"Yes, I have," the colonel said, smiling. Josh did not look up to see him smile. "Good night, then, Joshua."

Absorbed in his reading, Josh didn't answer.

The days grew colder. In December, both sides stopped fighting and built permanent winter camps, settling down to wait for spring.

Josh and his friends went into the forest and chopped down small trees, stripping the branches to make log houses, which they sealed with mud to keep out the freezing wind. Josh had a reasonably warm bed for the first time since he left Fort Ellsworth. Food was plentiful—fresh meat and vegetables and milk. His pants grew tight around the waist, and his legs stuck out at the bottom, so he was given a warm new uniform.

He taught his Maine friends how to play the game of "base-ball," which he had learned from the New Yorkers at Fort Ellsworth. They fashioned a bat from a sturdy oak branch and wrapped a ball of string with a leather glove sewn up tight. Sergeant Wallace said he felt like a fool running around the bases, so he stood behind home plate to stop fights that erupted over whether a pitch was good and whether a runner was safe or out.

The mutineers taught Josh how to play poker and how to keep an expressionless "poker face" when he was gambling. They laughed uproariously when he won with a bad hand because they could not tell that he was bluffing. He knew they let him win sometimes, but he didn't care and used his winnings for books and candy from the sutler's store.

The camp doctors were glad to have his help in the hospital. Although there were no battle wounds, there were stomachaches and fevers, and black eyes and broken bones from fistfights and playing "base-ball." Dr. Shaw showed Josh pictures in his big medical books and taught him how to splint a broken arm and where to press to stop bleeding. He told Josh of new studies in France that proved the importance of a doctor's washing his hands and using clean water and bandages on a wound. Josh told the doctor about the time he had used a Zouave's dusty coat to wrap the soldier's wounded leg.

"Do you suppose it made him sick?" he asked.

"If a dusty coat is all you have, it's better than letting a man bleed to death."

When Colonel Chamberlain returned to camp from Washington, where he had spent the winter months, he handed Josh a small book, explaining that he had liked it when he was young.

"I have seen you reading and thought you might enjoy these legends of the ancient heroes of Greece—Jason and the Argonauts, and Theseus, who slew the Minotaur."

"Thank you, sir," Josh said. "That was thoughtful of you."

"Perhaps we can discuss the stories when you've read them," the colonel suggested.

"Uh . . . well . . . yes, sir." Josh wasn't sure how it would be, discussing adventure stories with the colonel.

When he returned the book, Colonel Chamberlain asked eagerly, "Did you enjoy the stories, son?"

"Well, yes, sir, but I think Jere would have enjoyed them more. He always loved adventure. Reading these reminded me of him."

"I would like to have known your brother. He sounds a great deal like me at fifteen," the colonel said.

"I think you're still that way, sir," Josh blurted out. "You enjoy all this." He gestured to the soldiers sprawled beside the fires, the flags and tents, which were almost hidden in the evening mists.

"Yes, I do, Joshua. It's different from my life before the—"

"Colonel. Colonel Chamberlain," a voice called urgently. "There's a message just arrived from General Grant."

"We'll talk more later, Joshua. Come along. I may need you," the colonel said, hurrying off. He was smiling.

"That's what I mean, sir," Josh muttered as he followed the colonel.

In June, fighting raged near the mouth of the James River. General Grant pushed hard to cut the railroad lines bringing supplies from North Carolina to the Confederate capital at Richmond. The city of Petersburg was the hub of those railroad supply lines.

On June 18, Colonel Chamberlain was ordered to lead his soldiers in an attack south of Petersburg. Striding back and forth in front of his men, the colonel spoke of courage and sacrifice.

"We must cross that valley." He pointed to a narrow swamp below them. "Some will fall. It may be you or I. But we must go forward together." Drawing his sword, he moved down the hill.

With bayonets fixed, the soldiers followed him until they reached the swampy valley below. Sword raised, the colonel led them straight into the Confederate guns. Like Theseus moving forward to slay the Minotaur, Josh thought. Cannon exploded, and muskets burst into fire. In the first volley, a bullet struck the colonel's hip and passed through his body from one side to the other. He drove his sword into the ground and tried to remain standing, then dropped to one knee, and finally slumped down on the ground.

Josh watched in horror, then ran forward, pulling off his coat and pressing it to the gaping wound in the colonel's side.

A dusty coat is better than letting a man bleed to death, he remembered.

With a soft moan, the colonel ordered, "Go along and find another to help, Joshua. I am mortally wounded."

"No, sir, I will not," Josh answered.

A cannon shell fell next to them, exploding the earth outward and raining rocks down on them. Josh covered the colonel's head with his body to protect it and buried his own head in his arms.

When the shelling moved away across the valley, he whispered, "I'll be back," and clawed his way up the hill, crying out to the first officer he came to, "Captain! Captain! They have shot Colonel Chamberlain. He's dying."

The captain ordered his men to follow Josh and bring the colonel back on a stretcher, but when they reached him, the colonel's voice was barely a whisper. "Take care of the others. I am done for."

The stretcher bearers lifted him as gently as they could and carried him up the hill to the hospital.

Josh searched for more than an hour before he found Lieutenant

Chamberlain and Dr. Shaw and brought them to the hospital. They conferred with the doctors, who spoke in hushed tones and shook their heads.

Josh slumped to the floor outside the door of the colonel's room, crying silently, This is not an adventure, sir. Not now! His lips moved, whispering the words of the Twenty-Third Psalm. "Yea, though I walk through the valley of the shadow of death, I will fear no evil, for thou art with me. . . . " Please, God, walk with him through this shadow of death, he prayed.

The following day, Dr. Shaw took Colonel Chamberlain to the hospital at Annapolis, Maryland. By the time Josh returned to camp, the soldiers of the Twentieth Maine had heard that their colonel was near death. They tried to comfort each other, not ashamed of their tears. In sorrow, Josh wrote Mattie, telling her about the colonel.

> Every one among us loved him and would have followed him anywhere. I hardly knew our father, and The Man was never much of one to me, so if I could choose any man to be my father it would be this man. He helped me find a place in the war and showed me that I am the one who must decide what is right for me. From talking with the other men, I realize they feel the same about him, and we despair to think that we have lost him.
>
> Please pray for him, for all of us, and for your brother,
>
> Josh

After several weeks, when no bad news came from Dr. Shaw, they began to hope. Then, one day, the doctor returned, saying cheerily, "Good news, Joshua. The general is recovering nicely from his wounds."

"The general?"

"Yes. General Grant promoted Colonel Chamberlain to brigadier general as he lay near death. I think that is why he refused to die. He wanted to pin on that star."

"Are you serious?"

The doctor answered with a smile. "It was the kind of medicine you don't read about in books. And he had good care from the very start, when you wrapped his wound with your dusty coat."

★★ *Fourteen* ★★

CAPTURE

DURING the long summer and fall of 1864, the Union and Confederate armies circled each other, jabbing and retreating, like a pair of schoolboys fighting on the playground.

Josh was busy helping the doctors treat the wounded and dying. At night, he studied Dr. Shaw's big medical volumes by candlelight, struggling with the technical words and memorizing diagrams. His hands became steady and sure, and his manner was gentle, almost tender, with both Yankee and Rebel patients.

When General Chamberlain returned to camp from his convalescence, Josh watched him closely.

"I don't need help," the general snapped when Josh reached out to steady him.

"No, sir," Josh answered and continued to stay close by.

The snows came, and again the armies broke off fighting and hunched down in winter camps, protecting themselves against the cold.

By the spring of 1865, the Confederates had grown weak. Pursued relentlessly by the Union Army and cut off from food and ammunition, they nonetheless fought on.

Late in the afternoon of April 4, Josh waited as General Chamberlain finished a carefully worded message for General Grant.

A captain standing nearby spoke impatiently, "We've been at Jetersville all day, and there's no word from Grant. We need to move against the Confederates."

A young lieutenant spoke excitedly. "We have to have reinforcements *now!*"

"General Grant has promised two more corps by tomorrow," the general explained.

"We need them sooner if we're to cut the Danville Railroad lines," the captain fretted.

"General Lee will escape to North Carolina if we don't surround him. He mustn't get away!" The young lieutenant gestured wildly, jarring the little table, spilling the ink.

Patiently, General Chamberlain took a clean sheet of paper, saying, "We'll hold one more night where we are and move forward by dawn's first light. I shall write General Grant that we must have those reinforcements by dawn tomorrow. Joshua, this will be ready within the hour if there are no more floods of ink. You know where General Grant's headquarters are now?"

"Yes, sir." Josh smiled at the young lieutenant's embarrassment.

The general began his message again, finally folding it and sealing it with wax. "Be careful out there, son. There are Rebel soldiers everywhere. You'll need to move without attracting attention," he cautioned.

"But quickly," the young lieutenant added.

"Don't take chances, Josh. The Rebs are desperate now." The captain put his hand on Josh's shoulder.

When they had finished advising him, Josh slipped quietly out of camp in the direction of General Grant's headquarters. After a while, he stopped to rest and watched a flock of Canada geese foraging in a nearby field. His thoughts wandered back to the farm.

"What are you doing, boy?" a soft voice drawled behind him. Whirling around, Josh saw three figures standing in the trees. He stared at them stupidly.

"What are you doing, Yankee?" the voice repeated impatiently.

"I . . . I don't know," Josh stammered.

The man came close, peering curiously at him. Josh saw he wore a Confederate uniform with sergeant's stripes on the sleeve. But there was something different about the uniform. It didn't look like any he had seen before.

"What do you mean you don't know?" the sergeant snapped, his voice no longer soft.

"I'm lost, sir," Josh faltered, wondering whether it would work again.

"What're you lost from?" a younger soldier said, coming up to join the sergeant.

"I've lost my r . . . r . . . regiment." Josh stammered.

122

"What regiment is that, Yankee?"

"The Twentieth Maine," Josh answered truthfully. "We were camped by a creek, and I went for a walk . . . "

"Why'd you do that? Why'd you go for a walk?" The sergeant's voice cut Josh sharply.

"In the woods?" the young soldier shot at him.

Josh hung his head and said nothing.

"You're not lost, are you, Yankee boy?" A third soldier who had stayed in the trees sauntered out to join the group. "You ran away, didn't you?"

Josh looked down, digging the toe of his boot into the moldy leaves at his feet, twisting uncomfortably. " I . . . I . . . " He cowered, head down, digging his toe deeper into the leaves.

"We got ourselves a little Yankee deserter," the sergeant chuckled.

"Do the Yanks use boys to fight their war now? Have all the *men* been killed?" the young soldier taunted.

"I'm a drummer, sir," Josh whispered.

"You don't say. Well, come on. We'd better get you back to camp," the sergeant decided. "We don't want you to get eaten by 'bay-uhs' out here in the woods."

The soldiers laughed, pushing Josh roughly between them and setting off into the woods.

Something's not right, Josh thought. What is it?

As he trotted to keep up, he eased his hand toward his coat pocket, very slowly so that he didn't attract attention. The soldiers ignored him, laughing and crashing through the underbrush. Josh slipped the general's message out of his pocket in the palm of his hand, trotting along for a while holding the folded page. Then, very slowly he raised his hand to his mouth and slipped the message inside.

Hurrying to keep up, he chewed the message. The wax was hard now and sweet-tasting, like taffy, sticking in his teeth. He drew more and more saliva into his mouth to make a paste of the paper. Good practice, all those hardtack biscuits, thought Josh. When he was finally able to swallow the message, he gasped and sputtered to keep from gagging.

"What's the matter, Yankee drummer boy? We walking too fast for you?" The soldiers hooted, pushing Josh ahead of them roughly.

They finally reached a clearing where groups of soldiers squatted around several small fires, cooking, joking. A friendly scene.

"Look what we got," the young soldier hollered as they entered the camp. "We found ourselves a runaway Yankee drummer boy." The men looked up from the fire, studying Josh closely.

"How d'you know he's a drummer boy?" one of the soldiers by the fire asked, getting up, stretching, ambling toward them.

"Says he is."

"How d'you know he's telling the truth?"

"You wouldn't lie to us, would you, boy?" The young solder pressed his face close to Josh's.

Josh's stomach fell to his boot tops. *What if they don't believe me? What will they do to me?*

A tall, hollow-cheeked captain came out of the shadows and stood in front of him, looking him up and down. Scratching his beard, he circled Josh.

It's like playing cards, Josh thought. *Keep a poker face.*

"Search him," the captain snapped.

The sergeant reached into Josh's pockets and pulled out hardtack and some candy, which he tossed to the men at the fires. He patted and poked Josh until he was satisfied that was all the boy had.

"Nothing else," he told the captain.

"Samuel. Come on over here and bring that infernal drum of yours," the captain called. His voice was deep and lazy, dragging over the word "here," taking away the "r" so it sounded like "he-uh."

"Yes, sir, Captain," a cheerful voice answered, and a boy, smaller than Josh, appeared from the shadows. His smooth, black skin glistened in the firelight. He carried a brightly decorated drum half as big as he was.

"Give that Yankee your drum, Samuel," the captain ordered. Turning to Josh, he said, "Let's hear you play something for us."

Josh took the drum from Samuel and slipped the harness over his shoulders. With a flourish, he brought the drumsticks down softly and tapped out the rhythm of "The Battle Hymn of the Republic," whistling so the others could not hear. Finishing with a dramatic roll of sound, he tapped a marching cadence on the metal edge.

"All *raht,* all *raht,*" the captain drawled. "You're a fine drummer. You better pay attention, Samuel, or we'll trade you for this Yankee." Laughing at his joke, the captain turned away.

"Where are you from, sir?" Josh blurted out.

The captain whirled around, his laughter gone. "Why do you want to know, boy?" His voice curled around Josh like a whip.

"Because you talk funny," Josh babbled. "You say *raht* instead of right. All *raht*, all *raht*. It sounds funny." He smiled up at the captain, his eyes wide and innocent.

"He sounds like you, all *raht*, Cap'n Jessup," the sergeant chuckled.

"*Ah'um* from No'th Ca'lina, boy," the captain said more pleasantly, making his drawl thick and slow. The sergeant giggled.

"You sit *raht* over *they-uh*," the captain exaggerated his words, "while we *dee*cide what to do with you. Come along, Sergeant. We better get that message off to General Johnston *raht* now. He has some distance to travel if he's going to reach General Lee in time." They walked away laughing.

Josh handed the drum back to Samuel with a "thank you" and moved to the edge of the clearing. Dropping to the ground, he leaned his back against the trunk of a large tree. The soldiers around the campfire ignored him, so he gradually eased himself around the base of the tree until he faced into the woods, where he waited in the dark, unnoticed. After a while, he slipped away into the darkness, crawling on his hands and knees until he could no longer hear voices. Standing up then, he ran as fast as he could.

An hour later, he arrived, breathless, at General Grant's camp and gasped out the password. A guard took him to the entrance of the general's tent, where Josh spoke to one of the colonels he recognized.

"Sir. Colonel Roberts, sir."

"Joshua Parish, isn't it? General Chamberlain's messenger. Do you have a message for us?" Colonel Roberts asked.

"Yes, sir, but I swallowed it."

"You swallowed it?" Colonel Roberts hooted, turning to the officer next to him. "Get this boy something to eat, Lieutenant. He must be mighty hungry to eat General Chamberlain's fine words."

Serious again, he turned back to Josh. "Why did you eat the message, Joshua?"

"Well, sir, when the Confederates got me—" Josh began.

"The Confederates got you?" Colonel Roberts exploded.

"Some Confederate soldiers caught me, and I ate the message, and they asked me who I was, and their captain was from North Carolina, and he went off to send a message to General Johnston, so I slipped away and I—"

"Slow down, now. I want you to slow down and start again. Now tell me—Captain, come over here and listen to this," Colonel Roberts interrupted himself, motioning to one of General Grant's aides. "Tell us exactly what happened. Slowly."

"Yes, sir," Josh began. "I was bringing General Grant a message from General Chamberlain about the reinforcements he needs—"

"You read the message?" The aide's voice disapproved.

"No, sir, I heard them talking while General Chamberlain was writing the message."

"Go on, Joshua. Don't leave anything out," Colonel Roberts said. "You knew what the message said before you left General Chamberlain's camp. How long was it before you were captured by the Confederate soldiers?"

Joshua told his story slowly, careful not to leave out any detail. As he was speaking, General Grant came out of his tent and stood beside Colonel Roberts. When Josh had finished, the officers asked him questions. Over and over they asked him, "Are you sure he was from North Carolina?"

"Yes, sir. No'th Ca'lina was how he said it."

General Grant's stern eyes bored into him, searching for the truth. "You're certain he said he was sending a message to General Johnston."

"Yes, sir, I'm sure he said General Johnston."

"This boy's the best there is," Colonel Roberts said quietly to General Grant. He turned to Josh and asked, "Do you know why it's so important that we be sure it was General Johnston?"

"I know that General Johnston is in North Carolina, sir, and that General Lee wants to join up with him so they can continue fighting," Josh answered.

"You are exactly right," General Grant said. "We must keep that from happening. That's why your news is so important."

He put his hand on Josh's shoulder. "You have done us a great service, Joshua. We were not expecting soldiers from North Carolina to be here. It means General Lee is expecting reinforcements. We cannot let that happen, can we?" General Grant returned to his tent, calling his officers to follow him.

A sergeant brought Josh a cup of scalding coffee, which he drank as he waited for the officers to come back. When they did, General Grant said, "You can ride back to your camp behind Captain Nelson. I have written General Chamberlain that his reinforcements are on the way. My compliments to the general. He has chosen an excellent messenger, Corporal."

"I'm Private Parish, sir," Josh answered.

"You are Corporal Parish now. I am giving you a promotion for your very brave heart and your level head. I think you may have saved us from several more months of war. I have written to explain this to General Chamberlain." General Grant shook Josh's hand and returned to his tent.

"You see, Corporal Parish," Captain Nelson explained as he mounted his horse and pulled Josh up behind him, "if General Johnston and his soldiers had gotten here to reinforce General Lee . . ." Josh didn't hear the rest. The captain's horse reared and plunged into the dense woods, leaping over a fallen tree and grazing the overhanging branches. Josh kept his head down and hung on tightly as they raced through the blurred trees.

Later, when the story got around camp, his comrades slapped him on the back and called him Corporal and made quite a fuss over him, giving three hip, hip, hurrays.

General Chamberlain handed him his promotion, written out and signed by General Grant, himself. "Thank you, Joshua. If by your actions you have shortened this war by even one day, you deserve this promotion and the thanks of all of us. You have, indeed, proved yourself worthy of high honor."

Reinforcements arrived, and the final game of hangman began. Over the next two days, the troops of the Union Army tightened the noose around the Confederates. They reached the little town of Appomattox on the morning of April 9. Storm clouds gathered, then the sun broke through, and the day became oppressively hot. A truce had been declared, and for two long hours soldiers of both armies hung about in little clusters, talking, waiting.

Suddenly, General Lee rode through the lines of Confederate soldiers, straight through town from the river. Although his face was sad and lined with fatigue, he held his head high. His hair and beard were silver. His elegant uniform was embroidered with gold braid, and a jeweled sword hung by his side. He passed so close that Josh could have touched the sweaty side of his white horse, Traveler.

In a few minutes, General Grant came from the opposite direction, unsmiling, his eyes fixed straight ahead. He wore his shirt open at the neck because of the heat. His dark head was covered with a wide-brimmed, soldier's hat, the black felt dusty like his uniform. He seemed a plain soldier beside the elegant General Lee as they rode together to Wilmer McLean's home. They dismounted there and strode across the porch into the house. At a small desk in the parlor, General Grant wrote out the terms of surrender by hand, and both generals signed. The long Civil War was over.

Three days later, General Chamberlain's First Division was given the honor of receiving the arms and battle flags of the defeated Confederate regiments. It would be the formal ceremony of surrender.

The general assembled his men along the road so they faced the Confederate camp on the opposite side of the river. The road was wet from an early-morning shower, and thunder clouds remained in the leaden sky. In the camp across the river, gaunt soldiers buttoned their tattered uniforms. Josh watched as eight or nine men came together and bent over a ragged flag. One man had a knife. When they separated, the flag was gone. Just a torn corner stuck out of one soldier's pocket. Another man was folding a jagged piece, which he slipped inside his shirt. They have divided up their battle flag rather than surrender it, Josh thought.

As they waited for the Confederates to come, General Chamberlain spoke to his men of the pride and deep disappointment of the soldiers who would march in front of them in a few minutes.

"No matter how bravely they fought, no matter how hopeless their cause, they will come before us now, worn and thin. We must not destroy their pride. We must, instead, welcome them back into the union of states."

Josh tried to understand what the general meant by his compassionate words. I guess they're not our enemies anymore, he thought. We're going to have to get along together now.

"And so we shall all stand without a cheer or word or whisper and hold our breath as if it were the passing of the dead." Having said this, the general mounted his chestnut horse and turned to face the slow-marching Confederates.

As the Confederate general rode abreast, General Chamberlain gave the command, "Carry Arms!" His men slapped their muskets to their shoulders in a salute to their defeated enemy. The Confederate general acknowledged the salute, pressing his sword to the toe of his boot. Passing on up the road, the tired soldiers laid down their rifles, stacked their cartridge boxes, and gave up their torn and blood-stained flags.

That evening, the general found Josh where he sat with his friends and said, "Come walk with me awhile. We may not have a chance to talk after today."

As they moved away from camp, down to the river, General

Chamberlain said, "Did you see how few there were of Pickett's men, who charged across the valley at Gettysburg? So few left today of a whole division, five thousand men. Did you recognize them, Joshua, and see how few there were? The rest lie buried in wide graves, their names unknown."

"You know, sir, when you talk like that you sound like my mother when she read to us from the Bible."

The general smiled. "As I started to tell you once, I have not always been a soldier. Before the war, I taught religion at Bowdoin College in Maine."

"So that's how you knew it was the Twenty-third Psalm."

The general nodded.

"How do you teach religion, sir? How do you teach something like that?"

"That is an interesting question, Joshua."

"Yes, but how do you?" Josh persisted.

"Well, sometimes you start by talking about what people have believed in the past. And you find out what your students think is the right thing to—"

"The way you and I talked after Gettysburg," Josh interrupted. "About fighting and what is right for each of us."

"Yes, like that. And you found what was right for you, didn't you?"

"Yes . . ." Josh hesitated. "I didn't keep Jere safe . . . but I did help others."

"And kept them safe," the general added.

"Yes, I did do that sometimes. At least I was useful."

"You have been more than useful. You have a gift for healing, Joshua. From what Dr. Shaw tells me, you have been studying as though to prepare yourself. For what, I wonder? Do you know what you will do now that the war is over?"

"Well, sir, I've never been to school. My sister likes it though. When I get back to Rochester, I expect I'll go."

"I believe you will like school, too."

"Then she and I might go west to Wyoming in the Western Territories," Josh continued.

"You will have many choices to make when you get home. I think you will choose wisely as you have done in this war. If I can assist you, if you should decide you want to go to college, you can write to me. I would be happy to help you if I can."

"Thank you, sir. I'll remember that."

"In any case, you could write to me sometime just to tell me how you like school and how you're getting along. I'd like to know what you decide to do."

"I'll do that, sir. I'll write to you sometimes."

"Thank you, Joshua."

They strolled back to the campfires, which had been lit in the twilight. The general went to his tent, and Josh sat by the fire talking for a while. Then he left his friends and sat down some distance away to think about the day and about what the general had said to him.

He thought of Jere, who would always be with him, and of the others he had helped when he could no longer help his brother. Are they my brothers, too?

He thought of what he had learned about the way men behave in war and about doctoring and about himself. He wanted to save it all so that he would not forget, so that he would have the memories with him always.

Reaching into his pocket, he took out his pencil and a sheet of paper and began to write.

AFTERWORD

O N April 14, 1865, five days after the surrender was signed at Appomattox, President Abraham Lincoln was assassinated by John Wilkes Booth. Following Lincoln's death, Vice-President Andrew Johnson was inaugurated president.

In July, Johnson reviewed the victorious Union troops as they marched down the broad avenues of the capital at Washington. The president invited General Chamberlain to join him in the reviewing stand as the Twentieth Maine passed by. Bands played, flags waved, and everywhere people cheered. The long and terrible war was over at last.

In September 1866, Joshua Lawrence Chamberlain was elected governor of Maine and served four terms. He then became president of Bowdoin College and, subsequently, a trustee of the college, a position that he held until his death in 1914.

ACKNOWLEDGMENTS

My appreciation to my husband, Bob, who has helped in every possible way and whose suggestions and criticism I value; to my brother, Bruce Wallace, for his support and help; to Judy Leff and her fifth-grade students Katie, Kellie, Kevin, Mia, Trevor, and Zach; to Diane and John Hewitson and Willy Ginaven.

Further appreciation to Meghan Lodge, administrator of the Rochester Historical Society; Susan Cumbry, curator of the Fort Ward Museum in Alexandria, Virginia; Peggy Sheils, docent at the Joshua L. Chamberlain Museum in Brunswick, Maine; the Serra Research Center of the San Diego Public Library; the staff of the national parks at Gettysburg, Fredericksburg, Petersburg, and Appomattox; and the visitors' program known as Lee's Retreat, sponsored by Amelia, Appomattox, Cumberland, Dinwiddie, Nottoway, and Prince Edward Counties in Virginia, by the city of Petersburg, and by the National Park Service.

GLOSSARY

adjutant—the officer who assists a commander by writing letters, sending messages

aide—a young officer who assists a colonel or a general, often acting as a personal servant

ambush—a surprise attack

artillery—large guns or cannon

bayonet—a knife-like weapon attached to the forward end of the barrel of a musket or rifle; used for hand-to-hand fighting

breastworks—defenses built of rocks or logs high enough for soldiers to stand behind and shoot at the enemy while remaining protected

cadence—the beat or rhythm of marching tapped out by a drummer

cadet—a young person training to be a soldier or an officer

color bearer—the soldier who carries the flag

colors—the flag carried by a military troop; the American flag carried in battle

Confederate—a person belonging to or sympathetic to the Confederate States of America

deserter—a soldier who leaves the army without permission

field promotion—a promotion given by a general to a soldier for extraordinary service on the field of battle

forage—to search for food or supplies in the countryside.

forage cap—a small military cap, low in front, usually with a small visor

hardtack—a flour and water biscuit baked hard so it was easy to carry and would not spoil quickly

jerky—meat cut in thin strips and dried so that it wouldn't rot

Johnny Reb—a nickname given to Confederate soldiers

maneuver—planned movement of military troops

Glossary

mess—a military meal or the place where it is prepared and served

minié ball—a kind of bullet used in Civil War muskets

mortally wounded—hurt so badly that death is a certainty

musket—a long, smooth-bored, muzzle-loading firearm used during the American Civil War

mutineers—soldiers who refuse to obey orders

pickets—soldiers positioned around a military camp to guard against an attack

pontoon bridge—a bridge made of planks that are laid across boats floating in the water

quartermaster—a military officer who provides equipment, clothing and supplies to the troops

Rebel—anyone supporting the Confederate cause, especially a soldier

recruit—(noun) someone who has just joined the military; (verb) to enlist someone for service in the military

renegade—a deserter who may continue to operate as a soldier on his own, without supervision

reveille—a bugle call sounded early in the morning to get soldiers up or call them together

route step—a style of marching where soldiers don't have to stay in step with each other or remain silent; good for moving long distances without a drum beat

secede—to withdraw from a group, such as the United States of America

secesh—a nickname given to a secessionist

secessionist—a person who lived in the states that seceded from the United States of America and sympathized with the Confederate cause during the American Civil War

skirmish—a fight between small groups of soldiers

staff— the officers who assist a commanding officer in making decisions and planning strategy

stockade—a military jail inside a fort or camp

sutler—a civilian salesman who sets up a small shop in a military camp, selling luxuries like soap and tobacco, books and candy

taps—the bugle call sounded at night to order lights out; also used today at the end of a military funeral

truce—a temporary cease-fire agreed to by both sides

Union—the United States of America

veteran—a soldier who has served a long time in military service

volley—a shower of many guns firing at the same time

Yankee—a person living in the northern states and supporting the Union in the American Civil War

Zouave—a soldier who wore a uniform similar to those worn by the French Foreign Legion including exotic red pantaloons and blue jackets. Both Union and Confederate armies had Zouave regiments in the American Civil War.

BIBLIOGRAPHY

Chamberlain, Joshua Lawrence. *The Passing of the Armies.* Gettysburg, Pennsylvania. Stan Clark Military Books, 1994.

Chamberlain, Joshua Lawrence. *Through Blood and Fire at Gettysburg.* Gettysburg, Pennsylvania. Stan Clark Military Books, 1994.

Ferguson, Ernest B. *Chancellorsville, 1863, The Souls of the Brave.* New York. Vintage Books, 1993.

Murphy, Jim. *The Boys' War.* New York. Clarion Books, 1990.

Robertson, James I., Jr. *Tenting Tonight: The Soldier's Life.* Alexandria, Virginia. Time-Life Books, Inc., 1984.

Shaara, Michael. *The Killer Angels.* New York. Ballentine Books, 1974.

Tunis, Edwin. *Frontier Living.* New York. HarperCollins, 1976.

Trulock, Alice Rains. *In the Hands of Providence.* Chapel Hill, North Carolina. University of North Carolina Press, 1992.

Wallace, Willard M. *Soul of the Lion.* New York. T. Nelson, 1960.

Wheeler, Richard. *Witness to Gettysburg.* New York. Meridian, 1989.